RUPERT

THE RUPERT BEAR DOSSIER

Following Rupert Bear, his chums, his artists,
his writers and the world he lives in

By Brian Stewart   *Design* Howard Smith

*"The adventures allow each reader
to dream a little, laugh a little and to
ask for more Rupert"*

Nance Irvine - relative of Mary Tourtel

HAWK BOOKS

THE RUPERT BEAR DOSSIER
FIRST EDITION

ISBN 1 899441 65 4

PUBLISHED BY
HAWK BOOKS
SUITE 309, CANALOT STUDIOS
222 KENSAL RD., LONDON W10 5BN

Dossier Contents

This book is dedicated to the current Rupert team of Ian Robinson, John Harrold and Gina Hart, whose hard work is delighting so many children.

Acknowledgements

I would like to thank the Rupert staff of the *Daily Express*, both past and present, for answering so fully my correspondence. They have been most kind.

John Beck, a leading Rupert historian and collector, has been enormously helpful over many years, and he kindly read the manuscript of this book, making useful suggestions and improvements.

Neil and Paul Mattingly have been extremely generous with the loan of materials and a large number of the books illustrated are from Paul's collection. I am most grateful to Chris Beetles Gallery, London for the loan of many of Mary Tourtel's earlier panels. Peter and Sheila Blackburn have been equally kind, lending their collection of Rupert merchandise and ephemera. Mike Blisset has done a superb job on the photography of the collections.

Martin Hamer, an important dealer in 20th century children's books and comics, has also assisted, and David Rose and Audrey Bateman, both of the Rupert and Canterbury Group have been very supportive over many years. The Followers of Rupert are wonderfully helpful to anyone with an interest in the little bear, and I would like to thank them for their help and access to their records and archives.

I am also most grateful to the following:

Caroline Bott, Gyles Brandreth, Richard Brown, John Burgess, David Cousins, Jenny, Dave and Boris Cross, Mervyn Cutten, Manda Gifford, Marit Hendiks, Mrs Pat Hume, Nance Irvine, Brigitte Istim, Shelagh Jones, Mr and Mrs Chris Laming, Sir Paul McCartney, Margaret McCance, Carole Makeham, Steven Marshall, Mabel Matthews, Prof Alan Murray, Eleanor Newton, George Perry, Ken Reedie, Shirley Reeves, Anita and Eric Rigden, Tony Shuker, Steve Silk, Lawrence Stewart, Dr and Mrs Stewart and Geoffrey Warner.

Finally I would like to thank the designer Howard Smith and the publisher Patrick Hawkey for helping to make this project so much fun.

Nice words about Rupert

A Foreword by Gyles Brandreth

author, broadcaster, formerly the Member of Parliament for the City of Chester and a Lord Commissioner of the Treasury, is the founder of the Teddy Bear Museum in Stratford-upon-Avon and a life long Rupert fan.

For me Rupert is one of the giants of children's literature. I've been a Rupert fan ever since I can remember - certainly ever since I could read. As a child my favourite books, bar none, were my Rupert Annuals. I loved the characters, the stories, the whole world of Rupert. I used to try to learn the verses off by heart!

In 1988, when my wife and I founded the Teddy Bear Museum in an Elizabethan house in Stratford-upon-Avon, we created a Hall of Fame, a special oak-beamed gallery designed to honour those bears who have their paw prints in the sands of history. There was no question that Rupert had to have pride of place in our Hall of Fame. One of the features that Rupert fans find of particular interest are our old Annuals, especially the ones dating from the Second World War and produced under strict paper restrictions.

In Rupert Mary Tourtel created one of the great immortals of childhood and I salute her genius! What she originated, and Alfred Bestall sustained so brilliantly, wasn't simply a delightful bear with a special personality, it was a whole imaginative world. One day, I'm hoping to move there!'.

Gyles Brandreth

Rupert Bear's creator, Mary Tourtel, in the High Street at Canterbury.

RUPERT - the loveable bear from Nutwood is eight years older than Mickey Mouse, six years older than Winnie the Pooh and forty years older than young Paddington!

He was in fact the very first really famous bear.

For as long as people can remember, the Rupert annuals have continued to jump straight into the best sellers lists, and at Christmas the new annual can always be found in the top three. His image has appeared throughout the world in books, videos and merchandise and he is known in Abu Dhabi, Algeria, America, Australia, the Bahamas, Belgium, Ceylon, Chile, Denmark, Fiji, Finland, France, Germany, Greece, Holland, Hong Kong, Iran, Israel, Italy, the Ivory Coast, Japan, Kenya, Kuwait, Lebanon, Malaysia, Malta, New Zealand, Pakistan, Portugal, Sierra Leone, Singapore, Spain, Sweden and Zambia. He is Bruintje Beer in Holland, Rukas in Portugal and Rupert L'Ours in France, but he also appears in foreign countries untranslated to help teach English as a foreign language.

He was created in 1920 by a Canterbury lady, Mary Tourtel. His arrival was the result of a circulation battle in the British press. The *Daily Mail* was the first to make a serious bid to capture a child readership, producing the popular Teddy Tail in April 1915, drawn by Charles Folkard. The *Sketch* introduced Uncle Oojah early in 1919 written by Flo Lancaster and drawn by Thomas Maybank, and later that year the

Little Lost Bear. BY MARY TOURTEL

No. 1.—Mrs. Bear sends her little son Rupert to market.

Two jolly bears once lived in a wood;
Their little son lived there too.
One day his mother sent him off
The marketing to do.

She wanted honey, fruit, and eggs,
And told him not to stray,
For many things might happen to
Small bears who lost the way.

Rupert first officially appeared in the Daily Express on Monday 8 November 1920. A slightly smaller bear, he looked as if he was still wearing a nappy.

Daily Mirror responded with Pip and Squeak (later joined by Wilfred) written by Bertram J.Lamb (Uncle Dick) and drawn by Austin B.Payne.

The *Daily Express* decided to create a popular strip of their own and Rupert made his first official appearance on Monday 8 November 1920. He more than exceeded everyone's expectations!

No one could have imagined that he would go on to capture the imagination and affection of the nation for the rest of the century.

Drawn by Mary Tourtel from Rupert Little Bear's Adventures Number Two, published in 1924.

The Adventures of Rupert, The Little Lost Bear, by Mary Tourtel published in 1921 by Thomas Nelson and Sons. It was the first Rupert Bear book. Courtesy of Hamer 20th Century Books, Worksop.

This was no more evident than during World War II. Paper rationing had reduced the newspaper to a single sheet, but there was still room for Rupert in most of the issues. The proprietor, Lord Beaverbrook, felt that to remove him would damage national morale - and he was probably right! His enchanting world provided the ideal escapism from atrocities of the time.

Since his début millions of Rupert books have been sold and his image has been used on countless products. Songs about him have been recorded and he has starred on television and in the theatre. He is now a national institution and a multi-million pound industry.

The original Rupert by Mary Tourtel first appeared in black and white, and with scarf, sweater, check trousers and sturdy shoes. However, he was more like a real bear standing on its hind legs and when he appeared in colour on the covers of early books, his jersey was blue and his scarf grey.

As colour printing improved, and competition in children's books became more intense, Rupert was given an image with more impact, and he adopted the bright red and yellow clothes originally given by Mary Tourtel to Rupert's friend, Bill Badger.

Mary Tourtel flung Rupert into a fairy-tale world of magic spells, ogres and flying witches, dragons and wicked wolves. The scenes often took place in a timeless wonderland, with the 20th century mixed in a neat cocktail with the medieval, no doubt inspired a little by her native Canterbury.

His first adventures included his pals Bill Badger, Algy Pug, Edward Trunk, Podgy Pig and the Wise Old Goat, and usually ended in a predicament that kept young readers in suspense until the arrival of the following day's newspaper.

The first book in which Rupert officially appeared was *The Adventures of Rupert the Little Lost Bear*. It was published by Thomas Nelson in 1921 at 2 shillings (ten pence), and although the reproduction of Mary's fine work is rather crude it still has much charm.

Courtesy of Chris Beetles Gallery, London

From Rupert Goes to School , 1922 by Mary Tourtel.

The second of Rupert Little Bear's Adventures by Mary Tourtel, first published in 1924 by Sampson Low, Marston and Co, Ltd.

The first of Rupert Little Bear's Adventures by Mary Tourtel. It was first published in 1924 by Sampson Low, Marston and Co. Ltd

Further books in the series quickly followed, again reproducing previously published newspaper adventures. They were *The Little Bear and the Fairy Child*, *The Little Bear and the Ogres* and *Margot the Midget and the Little Bear's Christmas*.

When Rupert began his illustrious career he could be quite naughty at times! Here he is heading for trouble in "Rupert goes to School," 1922 by Mary Tourtel. The blue crayon did not register when making the printing plates and was an indication for the printer to lay a colour.

Sampson Low began publishing *Rupert Little Bear Adventures* from 1924 and the famous yellow covered Little Bear Library series began in 1928 priced one shilling. These were extremely popular although the reproduction of Mary's fine drawings was rather poor. Rupert also appeared in The *Daily Express Children's Annual* from 1930 onwards, sometimes in pop-up form *(see page 23).*

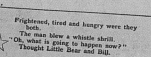

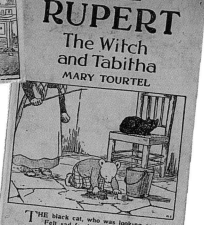

The Rupert Little Bear Library Series were published from 1928 by Sampson Low, Marston & Co. Ltd

In 1932 Stanley Marshall (known to the children as Uncle Bill) was given the task of forming 'The Rupert League'. To join readers had to collect six enrolment forms and send them with three penny stamps to the *Daily Express*. In return they received a lapel badge of Rupert's head, a birthday card, and membership forms. A medal was awarded to everyone who recruited ten others to the League. The aims of "The Rupert League" echoed the sterling qualities of the little bear.

Every child's letter was meticulously answered, and a roomful of staff was recruited to help with the task - reportedly costing the *Daily Express* £3000 a week - big money in those days!

In 1935 Mary Tourtel retired, and her talented successor Alfred Bestall took Rupert into a new age of adventures. After a few of the first Bestall strips, the *Daily Express* featured a previously commissioned series in puppet form, reproduced from photographs. The experiment was unsuccessful and Rupert returned to his drawn format.

Alfred Bestall eventually created over 270 Rupert adventures. When Alfred eventually found his work load too much, Enid Ash, Alex Cubie and Lucy Matthews were drafted in to help with the drawing, often producing figures for Alfred to complete the heads. He retired in 1965, when Cubie emerged as his successor, but Alfred still contributed occasional artwork until 1982.

"Members are to be cheerful, unselfish and to strive with all their might to make people happy. They should always be ready to do a good turn and especially to those less fortunate than themselves. They will always respect their elders and always cheerfully assist the aged or crippled and take particular care of little children".

Rupert expected high standards from the children who joined The Rupert League in 1932! Above is the Rupert League's Code of Conduct.

Rupert drawn by Mary's successor Alfred Bestall and coloured by Doris Campbell. Improvements in colour printing allowed Rupert to enter a new era.

In turn, after producing a number of adventures, the gifted John Harrold established himself as the official Rupert artist, first illustrating the stories of James Henderson and then those of Ian Robinson.

John has been drawing Rupert now for over twenty years - and the outstanding quality of his artwork has won him, like his predecessors, an important place in British book illustration.

Under each era Rupert's appearance may have changed, but his character remains basically the same, always brave and adventurous, modest and honourable. Comradeship and helping others is important to him - and right always seems to prevail in the end.

Below: Drawn by John Harrold and coloured by Gina Hart from the 1996 Rupert Annual

RUPERT AND TEA

Drawn by Mary Tourtel from Rupert.. and the Old Miser, published in 1925.

Drawn by Alfred Bestall from the 1942 Rupert Annual

Drawn by John Harrold and coloured by Gina Hart from the 1996 Rupert Annual

Rupert's Who's Who

Drawn by John Harrold from the 1984 Rupert Annual.

Rupert has so many friends and knows so many people that if this is your first Rupert Annual you may be a bit puzzled to begin with. So to help you, let's introduce some of the people you will meet or hear about, although one or two of them make only a very brief appearance in this book. Here they are —

ALGY PUG. Another very close chum who has shared a great many of Rupert's most exciting adventures. At times just can't resist playing tricks.

BILL BADGER. A very close pal. Easy-going. Can take a joke. Useful in a tight spot. Always looks on the bright side. One of Rupert's oldest friends.

BINGO. Very clever. Quite the inventor. Very curious and has to find out how things work. He is happy to go off on his own, but a good pal nevertheless.

PODGY PIG. Loves food. Doesn't like work. But even if he can be greedy and lazy sometimes, in the end he usually turns out to be good-hearted.

EDWARD TRUNK. Because he is so strong, a useful friend. Like most strong people he is really rather gentle. Always cheerful and ready to help.

WILLIE MOUSE. Rather timid. He'd love to be adventurous like the others. But he isn't. He does keep on trying, though. And that is really being brave.

PONG-PING. Comes from China. Very rich. Very proud. At times he can be quick-tempered but is kind and generous. Owns a small pet dragon.

ROLLO. The gipsy boy. A close friend of Rupert for a long time. Brave, quick-thinking. Lives with his wise old Grannie in a caravan and travels quite a lot.

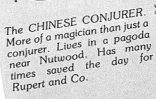

The CHINESE CONJURER. More of a magician than just a conjurer. Lives in a pagoda near Nutwood. Has many times saved the day for Rupert and Co.

The SAGE OF UM. Clever, genial, but just a bit dithery. Travels all over the world in his Brella. Rupert first met him during an adventure with the Chinese Conjurer.

The WISE OLD GOAT. Very clever. Helpful, kind but mysterious. No one is sure how long he has lived in his castle in the hills which he seldom leaves.

The PROFESSOR. Rupert's old inventor friend, does not appear in this book. His SERVANT does appear. But no one knows much about him at all.

Mr Anteater drawn by Alfred Bestall

Edward Trunk drawn by Mary Tourtel

Drawn by Mary Tourtel from Rupert Little Bear's Adventures Number Two, 1924

From 'Rupert goes to School', 1922 by Mary Tourtel

Rupert's Illustrators & Colourists

Mary Tourtel 1874-1948

The artist who created Rupert Bear, Mary Tourtel (née Caldwell), was born at 52 Palace Street, Canterbury on 28 January 1874, the daughter of Samuel Austen Caldwell and Sarah (née Scott). Mary was the youngest member of a very talented family. Her father designed and restored stained glass for Canterbury Cathedral and was followed into business by his son, also called Samuel, who continued caring for the cathedral glass for more than fifty years and was responsible for saving it from destruction from the blitz in World War II.

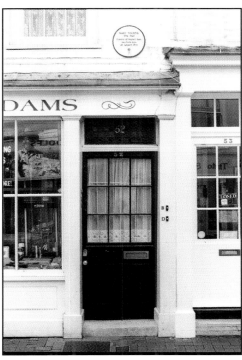

The birthplace of Rupert creator Mary Tourtel (neé Caldwell) at 52 Palace Street, Canterbury.

Another of Mary's brothers, Edmund Caldwell, was an animal painter of considerable talent, who exhibited at the Royal Academy and illustrated many children's books - including *Jock of the Bushveld*, which is still in print today.

Mary (far right) with her parents, two of her brothers, Sam and George, her sister Georgina and her sister's children.

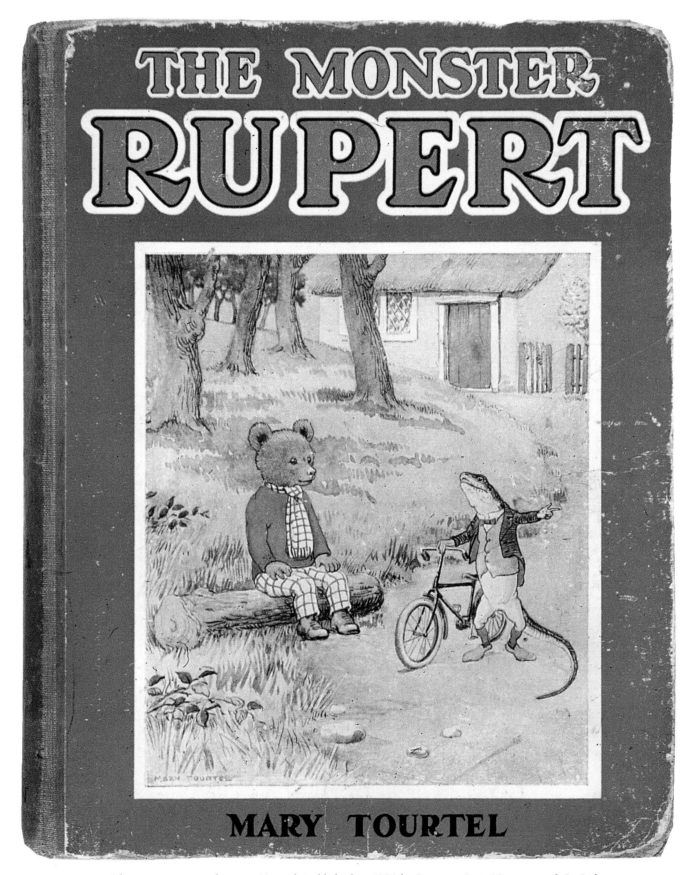

The Monster Rupert by Mary Tourtel. Published in 1932 by Sampson Low, Marston and Co. Ltd.
The lizard's bicycle has a very low saddle to accommodate his tiny back legs!

"Rupert is the best children's character in any newspaper anywhere in the world"

Lord Beaverbrook

The Sidney Cooper Gallery of Art, St Peter's Street, Canterbury. Mary trained in art here.

Three frames from "Rupert Goes to School", 1922 by Mary Tourtel.

Mary loved drawing from an early age. After attending the Simon Langton School for Girls between 1884-1889, where she was described as a shy and dreamy child. She trained at the Sidney Cooper School of Art in St Peters Street, Canterbury. Here she received tuition in landscape and animal painting from Britain's most accomplished cattle painter, Thomas Sidney Cooper CVO RA (1803-1902) and was clearly a most outstanding student. She won a holiday to Switzerland, and a number of medals for drawing. In 1891 she was awarded a National Bronze Medal and the Queen's Prize for Design for 'A Damask Hanging'.

The following year she was awarded a National Book Prize and in 1893, when Cooper himself awarded the prizes, she received three firsts, one for China painting, another for modelling and a third for the base relief of the Virgin and Child, described as '*the best work during the year in any stage of technical wor*k'. In 1894, when the Mayor of Canterbury made the presentations, she won the coveted 'Princess of Wales' scholarship and a Gold Medal. The Mayor of Canterbury distributed the prizes that year and told those present that these were the highest awards an art student could obtain 'and her splendid success reflected the highest honour both on herself and the School of Art'.

Other awards included The Rosa Bonheur Prize, and the Owen Jones Medal for a design in tapestry, competing with 11,000 other students. This medal could only be gained once in a lifetime.

She went on to study at the Royal College of Art between 1897-1900, and it was during this time that she met her future husband Herbert Tourtel. He was a young inspiring poet and was looking for a talented student to illustrate his poems. Mary was recommended to him and it was not long before their working relationship blossomed into romance. Privately, he called her Portia (daughter of the gods) and

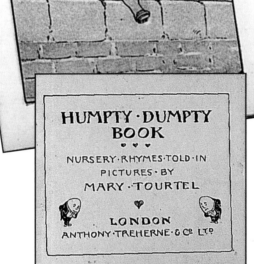

The Humpty Dumpy Book by Mary Tourtel, published in 1902 by Anthony Treherne & Co. Ltd.

she called him Juan. They married on 26 September 1900 in the church at Stoke Poges.

Mary was an excellent animal painter and she was commissioned to illustrate several children's books. Mary's first hardback was *A Horse Book* (number 10 in the Dumpy Books for Children) published by Grant Richards in 1901 . She also contributed book 21 in the series, entitled the *Three Little Foxes,* published in 1903 and featuring characters such as Old Bear Ogre, Mr Frog, and Queen Rabbit and her Royal Bodyguard of Bunnies, as well as two stump books in 1904, *Old King Cole* and *The Rabbit Book.*

Another of her books was the *Humpty Dumpty Book*, published by Anthony Treherne in 1902. The reproductions in these books were produced by Edmund Evans, one of the leading exponents of early colour printing, whose reputation had been made by his careful reproductions of the work of Walter Crane, Kate Greenaway and Randolph Caldecott.

The Rabbit Book - A stump book by Mary Tourtel published in 1904 by Anthony Treherne & Co. Ltd.

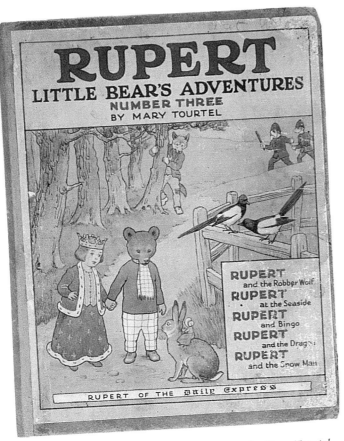

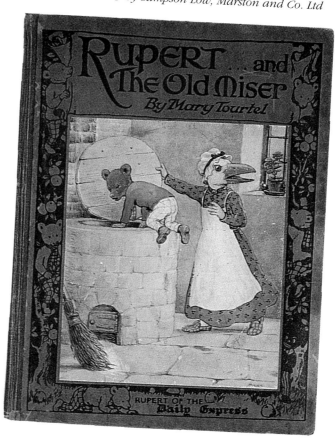

Below: Rupert and the Old Miser by Mary Tourtel.
Published in 1925 by Sampson Low, Marston and Co. Ltd

Above: Rupert Little Bear's Adventures No 3 by Mary Tourtel.
First published in 1925 by Sampson Low, Marston and Co. Ltd.,

From "Rupert Goes to School", 1922 by Mary Tourtel. Courtesy of Chris Beetles Gallery, London

Cover illustration for When Animals Work by Mary Tourtel - a suppliers book of handkerchiefs printed by Sefton Fabrics. © Canterbury Museums Collection.

Mary contributed features to both the *Daily Express* and the then recently launched *Sunday Express*. She was responsible for 'In Bobtail Land' 1919, which ran for six months, but perhaps most popular was the series of 'Animals at Work', which appeared the same year. Items from these features were produced as a superb set of handkerchiefs by Sefton (Canterbury Museums Collection) and were later reprinted in some of the Sampson Low Rupert publications. In amongst Mrs Porker, Mrs Quack, Mrs Baa, is what looks remarkably like a Mrs Bear and young Rupert, perhaps his first unofficial appearance.

IF HE HAPPENS TO SIDE-SLIP
THERE'LL BE SOME TO-DO
ALL THE STUFF WILL MIX UP IN A REAL IRISH STEW.

Detail of a handkerchief from When Animals Work by Mary Tourtel. The figures look remarkably like Rupert and his mother and possibly pre-date his first official appearance in the Daily Express. © Canterbury Museums Collection.

RUPERT AND THE BRIGANDS

So Rupert and the Little Man
  Ran downstairs once again;
They cleaned the place up, lit the fire,
  And worked with might and main.

Then Rupert searched the larder through;
  He found some mutton there,
And potatoes too. "We'll make a stew
  For the Pig," said Little Bear.

When all was nicely cooked they went
  Upstairs and tapped his door.
They found him sound asleep again,
  And, my, how he did snore!

From Rupert Little Bear's Adventures Number Two, by Mary Tourtel. Published in 1924 by Sampson Low, Marston and Co, Ltd.

By 1920 Herbert was a senior executive on the *Daily Express* and his editor, worried about the growing success of children's characters in rival newspapers, thought the *Daily Express* should produce an idea on similar lines. Mary, who was already well regarded for her animal sketches, was the obvious choice as illustrator. It was arranged that she would draw the pictures and write the stories and Herbert would help with the rhymes when he had the time.

On Monday 8 November 1920 Rupert made his first official appearance in the *Daily Express*. The adventure, entitled Little Lost Bear, occurred over 36 days, finishing shortly before Christmas, to enable the next story, Little Bear's Christmas, to remain topical.

Generally only one picture a day was used, but occasionally two and sometimes as many as four appeared. Mary also experimented with different shaped panels, which have considerable charm.

There were no plans to make Rupert an enduring figure, it was something that happened naturally. At times he would disappear from the paper altogether, his place being taken by another Mary Tourtel character called Margot, but as she told a fan in a letter written in 1926 from her residence at 36 Via Montebello, Florence:

"...I see you like Rupert better than Margot the Midget - I do too, and I am glad you like my stories. I am always so glad to know that my little readers like Rupert and his adventures. With much love and kisses and thank you again for your nice letter

Yours affectionately - Mary Tourtel'.

Mary and Herbert never had any children of their own. They were devoted to each other and enjoyed travelling. They went by steamship to Italy, Egypt and India, but it was Italy they loved best.

When Herbert developed heart trouble, Mary went with him to Italy and then to Germany where he entered a sanatorium at Bad Nanheim. On 6 June 1931 he died aged 57. Deeply distressed, Mary returned to England.

Above: Rupert and his Friend Margot, by Mary Tourtel, 1926. Published in a larger yellow format in 1926 by Sampson Low, Marston and Co. Ltd.

The Ogre orders Rupert to be locked up in the High Tower - a drawing my Mary Tourtel based on the West Gate, Canterbury. From The Adventures of Rupert - The Little Lost Bear by Mary Tourtel published in 1921 by Thomas Nelson and Sons, Ltd

She continued drawing Rupert for the *Daily Express*, but she began to find that her eyes were hurt by bright light, although this did not affect the quality of her drawing. She had moved to Llandrindod Wells, a town renowned for its medicinal springs. Eventually in 1935 she was forced to retire. Her last story was 'Rupert and Bill's Seaside Holiday' which ended on 27 June 1935. In her career she had contributed over 3500 pictures and at least eighty-seven Rupert stories to the *Daily Express* over a period of fifteen years.

From "Rupert Goes Hiking", 1932 by Mary Tourtel.

She returned to Canterbury and took accommodation at the Baker's Temperance Hotel. John Burgess was about ten years old when he first met her and remembers her as *"a tall lady with pearl earrings. She nearly always wore black clothing, which was possibly mourning clothing for her husband - as she missed him terribly. She was a very nice and interesting lady with plenty to say. She was kind with a wonderful sense of humour and she was full of life."*

Her best friend, Wilhelmina Ockenden, who she had known since her school days wrote '*Mary grew into a perfectly charming and beautiful woman. She was very reserved, and truly modest, and never sought publicity. She was also a real authority on antique furniture and old china. She gave much pleasure to many children through her drawings and in 'Rupert Bear' she sought to show that truth, kindness, unselfishness and courage counted for so much and were great things'.*

A Pop-Up by Mary Tourtel from The Daily Express Children's Annual, 1931

In 1948 Mary collapsed in the street from a brain tumour on her way to meet her friend, Wilhelmina, for lunch, and passed into a coma. She was taken to Canterbury Hospital, but never regained consciousness. She died there on 15 March aged seventy-four.

In her will she left money to the Newspaper Press Fund in memory of her husband, to the RSPCA, and to societies dealing with the prevention of cruelty to animals in Florence, Naples and Rome. She was cremated at Charing crematorium and her ashes buried in St Martin's churchyard, Canterbury, her desired place of rest. Her husband's ashes were removed from Golders Green crematorium, as she requested, and were buried with her.

It is only in recent years that she has gained the public recognition she so richly deserved. The artists that followed in her footsteps, however, have all admired her work. Alfred Bestall treasured a little drawing by Mary of Rupert riding in a coach and four and kept it in his collection throughout his life. John Harrold

From "Rupert Goes Hiking" 1932 by Mary Tourtel

adores her drawings and commented: "I have immense admiration for Mary's drawing, and believe her talent has been vastly underestimated. I am particularly impressed by her ability to draw a great variety of animals from various angles, demonstrating a thorough understanding of their characteristics, movements and dynamics". He also considers it a scandal that so much of her delicate artwork has been tampered with.

The grave of Mary and Herbert Tourtel in the churchyard of St. Martin's, Canterbury.

Indeed, her work has been strengthened, doctored, completely redrawn, reproduced by poor printing, and even forged. Her original artwork reveals her to be a gifted, imaginative and sensitive artist. Her characterisation was brilliant and she really seemed to breath life into her figures. It is perhaps this quality that has enabled other great illustrators to adopt her characters as their own and continue the Rupert story.

Wasdale Brown

In the early 1930's the *Daily Express* produced a children's supplement entitled *The Daily Express Children's Own*. Rupert was one of the main features, but Mary Tourtel was having trouble meeting the deadlines, and another artist had to be found to help out. The editor of the children's features, Stanley Marshall briefly employed Wasdale Brown, who worked as a staff member for Morley Adams. The supplement was short-lived, and after a few editions was dropped.

Alfred Bestall MBE
1892-1986

Alfred Edmeades Bestall took over from Mary Tourtel when she retired, and he wrote and drew the stories. Rupert could not have been left in better hands.

Alfred was born in Mandalay, Burma on 14 December 1892, the son of a Methodist minister, the Rev. Arthur Bestall, and his wife Rebecca (née Edmeades). They were pioneering missionaries there and did much work helping lepers.

Alfred was educated at local schools in Sheffield, North Shields and Southsea. From the age of twelve he attended Rydal School, Colwyn Bay (1904-11), and won a scholarship to the Birmingham Central School of Art which he attended 1912-14.

He volunteered for the Army Service Corps, and spent three and a half years serving in Flanders during World War I as a driver-mechanic with the 35th (Bantam) Division. From 1919 he attended the LCC Central School of Art evening classes, in his own words learning to be an "*illustrator and painter in oil, watercolour, line and wash*".

From 1920, with the help of his agent Graham Hopkins, he made his living contributing humorous illustrations to *Punch* (over an hundred drawings), the *Tatler* (over forty colour paintings), the *Bystander*, *Passing Show* and various other magazines. He also illustrated nearly fifty books, including some written by A.A.Milne, and at one time

designed the costumes and sets for Enid Blyton's *Twelve Plays for Children*. She was so pleased with it that she wrote to Alfred saying it is:

'The most perfectly illustrated book now on my bookshelf. I think every one of your drawings is exquisite and admirably suited to the childlike spirit I wanted to give to the plays".

On Mary's retirement in 1935, the *Daily Express* started looking for a suitable replacement to draw Rupert's continuing adventures. After testing several candidates for the job they were impressed by Alfred Bestall's selection of drawings and decided he was the perfect choice. However, there was little time as Mary's last story was shortly to come to an end. It was decided that there should be

Above: Alfred Bestall

The New Adventures of Rupert, 1936.
The start of the popular Rupert Annuals.

two panels each morning, with eighty words of narrative underneath. Alfred's first story, 'Rupert, Algy and the Smugglers', appeared on 28 June 1935.

The children's editor, Stanley Marshall, reminded him of the responsibility he owed the children:

'There must be no bad characters, no magic, no fairies."

Although, Bestall did not always keep to these rules, he did take his duties seriously:-

'I was always conscious of the responsibility I had when chronicling Rupert's adventures. The thought of Rupert being in people's homes and in so many children's heads was a perpetual anxiety to me".

Rupert with Bingo the Brainy Pup drawn by Alfred Bestall and coloured by Doris Campbell from the 1946 Rupert Annual. Bingo, invented by Bestall in 1945, was clearly a genius, but his schemes were not always successful. His teacher, Dr Chimp, commented: "I would have never have let Bingo learn science if I'd known he was going to blow the place up". Some Rupert Follower's believe that Bestall based the character of Bingo on himself!

Alfred cleverly introduced Rupert to a whole new world of fantasy. The little bear's adventures took him to every corner of the globe. His pals now included the Conjuror and Tigerlily, Bingo the Brainy Pup, the Professor and the Dwarf Servant, Billy Goat, Sailor Sam, Pong-Ping the Pekinese, Willy Mouse and a host of other characters and for the next thirty years he drew the daily panels and wrote the stories (although not the rhymes).

In 1981 Alfred recalled:

"A Rupert panel takes me about three hours from start to finish and I always tried to maintain a steady schedule of three panels a day in order that I keep ahead".

Besides creating over 270 Rupert adventures, many running considerably more than 40 panels, he also illustrated the Annuals from 1936. He officially retired in 1965 with his last story 'Rupert and the Winkybickies' ending on 22 July, but he was still persuaded to contribute some occasional artwork until 1982, when he was aged ninety. A unique feature of the annuals was the design of the endpapers with the settings of tropical islands, the flora and fauna of the seashore and the cloud-capped palaces. It was one of these endpapers that inspired Sir Paul McCartney to produce the BAFTA award-winning video Rupert and the Frog Song, which Alfred thought *"frightfully clever"* (see pages 78, 79 & 85).

Alfred also introduced the popular paper-folding features into the Annuals, which resulted in his election as President of the British Origami Society when he was 86.

Although he could be firm to his colleagues on the *Daily Express*, he was a kind and well-mannered man, always being polite to fans that sought him out and replying at great length to their letters. He could also be helpful and thoughtful to others, and spent many years devoted to his mother, who lived to be a hundred, and his handicapped sister.

His God-daughter, Caroline Bott, remembers:

'*He was gentle, courteous and kind and always appreciative. He seemed to see only the best in any person and any situation*'.

He spoke with a stutter, which in his youth was very extreme. However, he felt that, to a large extent, his ability to draw was nurtured and developed because of his immense difficulties in communicating vocally.

To an extent he was a delightful anachronism in a modern world. He would not sign his artwork in full until after Mary Tourtel had died, although occasionally he would sneak his initials in on a suitcase or trunk.

Left: Endpaper by Alfred Bestall from the 1973 Rupert Annual.

Alfred Bestall brought origami into Rupert's adventures. This panel, coloured by Doris Campbell, is from the 1946 Rupert Annual.

When James Henderson asked if he socialised with other illustrators he replied that he always declined because he was not *'one for lifting the elbow'*. In truth he was extremely shy.

At the *Daily Express* offices, where everyone knew each other on first name terms, he insisted on being called formally 'Mr Bestall'. Indeed, it came as something of a shock to James Henderson when, after years of working with him, he heard the artist being called 'Uncle Fred' by his God-daughter. Alfred loved being called Uncle Fred by her, it reminded him of the character in his P.G. Woodhouse books.

Rupert consoles Podgy Pig's mother in a panel drawn by Alfred Bestall , coloured by Doris Campbell, from the 1951 Rupert Annual.

When asked in an interview the secret of Rupert's success he replied:

'Fancy asking me! I don't know I am sure!. I can only hope that the overwhelming affection that I have for children possibly shows itself through the stories and therefore children accept it on that basis'.

In 1985 he was awarded the MBE and on his 93rd birthday he received a telemessage from Buckingham Palace.

Drawn by Alfred Bestall, coloured by Doris Campbell, from the 1975 Rupert Annual.

"I have heard you were sadly unable to receive your MBE in person from The Queen recently. I wanted to send you my congratulations on your award, and to wish you a very happy birthday with many returns. As a child I well remember your marvellous illustrations of Rupert Bear.
Charles."

Drawn by Alfred Bestall, coloured by Doris Campbell, from the 1953 Rupert Annual.

For all his success Alfred recognised Mary Tourtel's

important contribution to the Rupert story. He owned among his prized possessions an original Rupert drawing by Mary, and made the pilgrimage to Canterbury at the age of 87 to visit her grave, spending some time hunting for it in the long grass. He wanted to hear all about Mary and Herbert Tourtel from Mary's niece, Mabel Matthews. He wrote to her that year in 1980:

One of Alfred Bestall's prized possessions - a delicate pen and ink drawing by Mary Tourtel.

'*This November will mark the Golden Jubilee of Rupert and I don't know whether the Daily Express is planning any celebration. The new Rupert Annual is extra large for the occasion but it omits all reference to the "Jubilee" and from a Collector's point of view I fear the size is going to be unpopular.*

Although at my age I keep up very little drawing - only 3 pages, plus an Origami page this year - I can at least put in a report of my visit.

It is unthinkable that Mary should be forgotten on the sixtieth Birthday of her creation'.

Alfred in his old age was a constant concern to those at the *Daily Express*. He would readily admit to them that he would drop off to sleep at his drawing board, but would insist on driving his car between Surbiton and his Welsh cottage, Penlan in Beddgelert, albeit breaking the journey somewhere around Birmingham. However, the feared accident did not occur.

Below: Janet, Pauline and Beryl - the Nutwood Girl Guides based on real guides that Bestall knew. A drawing by Alfred Bestall and coloured by Doris Campbell from the 1953 Rupert Annual.

Below : As the workload became too great for Alfred Bestall other artists were called in to assist under his direction, with Alfred drawing key heads.

He spent his 93rd birthday in hospital in Caernarvon, suffering from cancer. He remained cheerful, teaching other patients origami. He was told by the consultant that he could never live alone at Penlan again. He said to his God-daughter, Caroline Bott: '*I had better give you Penlan now. You'll find my early artwork in the loft. You'll have to have a huge bonfire!*'.

He was transferred to Wern Nursing Home after Christmas and on 15 January 1986 he passed away. Throughout his life his art and his Christianity had remained his driving force. He was buried with his parents and sister at Brookwood in Surrey.

Fortunately his advice for a bonfire was not taken and these works are now lovingly cared for by his God-daughter, who is anxious that they should remain together. This outstanding collection forms a fitting tribute to Alfred - one of the finest illustrators of the 20th century.

Many of Alfred's stories were created at the kitchen table in his house in Surbiton between the hours of 6pm and 2 am. Sometimes his kitchen provided the inspiration for some of the drawings. Mrs Bear's wonderful Welsh dresser, for example, could be found there.

Above: The back cover of the 1964 Rupert Annual shows Alfred's cottage Penlan, in Beddgelert, North Wales. The front features the Snowdon Horseshoe.

Left: Alfred Bestall took this cottage at Beddgelert in North Wales in 1956 spending happy summers there. The view looks out on the River Glaslyn. In 1980 he left Surbiton to move to his cottage permanently.

Doris Campbell 1918 -1997

When in 1940 full-colour reproduction was intro-duced, Alfred Bestall was too busy to undertake this task. He reserved his colouring for covers and endpapers alone.

The colouring of the panels was given to professional colourists, the most important of whom was Doris Campbell, who was employed by Florence Studios as part of a team. Her colouring of Rupert started in 1945, and she produced such sensitive work, that she soon became the sole colourist.

Her husband was a retired head teacher, and after his death, Frank Parker, the books manager, decided it would be helpful to end the contract with the agency and give Doris the job as a freelance.

She coloured Rupert drawings for fifty years, including the work of Alfred Bestall, Enid Ash, Alex Cubie and finally John Harrold. The 1992 Rupert annual was the last one she coloured singlehandedly, the 1993 and 1994 annuals were completed with the help of Gina Hart.

Doris retired officially in 1995 and the *Daily Express* gave her a special presentation at her home in Bournemouth to mark her long association with Rupert. She died of pneumonia on 14 July 1997.

Doris's importance in the Rupert story cannot be overestimated.

John Harrold writes: *"I think Doris's forte was the beautiful evocative colouring of the Rupert landscape, which contributed so much to the magic of Nutwood for so many years. She had an ability to depict receding fields and hills with an infinite variety of clean, fresh and imaginative colours or to suggest a rich herbaceous border without, in fact, painting individual specific flowers - and of course those lovely graded skies, which are an important element of the Rupert enchantment".*

Colouring by Doris Campbell, drawn by Alfred Bestall from the 1968 Rupert Annual.

Colouring by Doris Campbell, drawn by Alfred Bestall from the 1949 Rupert Annual.

Colouring by Doris Campbell, drawn by Alfred Bestall from the 1953 Rupert Annual.

Arthur Joll b.1904.

Arthur Joll was born in Nottingham on 31 March 1904. He studied art at Northampton and worked as a commercial artist. He was employed by Greycaines, who were responsible for printing the majority of Rupert's annuals between 1936 and 1953. Like Doris he was employed in the early days to colour Alfred Bestall's stories, and always enjoyed helping to take part in the production of a Rupert book. He was foreman of the artists' department and camera room.

Drawn by Enid Ash and coloured by Doris Campbell from Rupert and Neddy - Adventure Series Number 12 April 1952.

Jennifer Miles

Another of the artists briefly employed to help Bestall meet his deadlines.

Enid Ash

She was employed to draw Rupert when Bestall's health began to suffer and Cubie was struggling to accomplish the Rupert style. She was very successful, but like so many artists she had difficulty with Rupert's head. A compromise was reached, and Bestall was employed to correct or draw Rupert's head.

*Drawn by Enid Ash and coloured by Doris Campbell from Rupert and Neddy - Adventure Series Number 12 April 1952.
Was P.C. Growler on holiday?*

Drawn by Enid Ash and coloured by Doris Campbell from Rupert and Neddy - Adventure Series Number 12 April 1952.

Alex Cubie 1911-1995

When Bestall's health became fragile, Alex Cubie was first employed to work on the Rupert Adventure series. When Alfred Bestall stopped producing the Rupert stories for the *Daily Express* in 1965, the job passed to Alex.

Alex had been a cartoon film animator with the Rank organisation and the influence of this work was noticeable in his strong cinematic compositions. He liked to mix the frames with distant, close up, and mid distance 'shot's' to give the images variety. By now the job of producing Rupert was split: Alex doing the drawings and the stories being created by Freddie Chaplain, a veteran of children's comics publishing.

Alex was born in Renfrew, near Glasgow on the 1 August 1911. His interest in art was encouraged at school.He began his professional life as an apprentice lithographic artist in Glasgow and produced cartoons for the *Glasgow Evening Citizen*.

He moved to London in 1934, where he worked in Fleet Street producing cartoons for the *Daily Sketch* and *The Leader*.

He was called up for service in the army in 1940, and trained as a fitter. On the discovery of his artistic skills he was transferred to an army all ranks design team, where he drew layouts for tactical exercises.

After the war he returned to London's Fleet Street, designing greetings cards, before joining Rank's studios in Cookham and the team for animated film production under the direction of Walt Disney's David Hand.

From about 1951 he worked for the *Daily Express* as a general

Alex Cubie at his home in Girvan May 1995. The photograph is courtesy of his close friends, Les and Val Sayer.

artist, but was later brought in to assist Alfred Bestall with the Rupert stories. He also produced a number of puzzles and magic painting pages. Alfred Bestall said that in his opinion Alex was the real expert when it came to puzzles, and he derived much pleasure from creating them.

He married in the 1950's and settled in Old Windsor. Following Alfred Bestall's retirement he designed covers and end papers for the Rupert annuals between 1974 - 1977.

In 1971 he moved to Girvan, where his holiday cottage at 25 Ballybroke Street became his permanent home. Alex was a well liked and respected figure. He offered assistance to many projects in the town; shop signs for Buttens Flower Shop and cards featuring Ailsa Craig to assist efforts towards an Ailsa Craig Visitor Centre in Girvan.

In draft reply to a letter from Professor Alan Murray of the Followers of Rupert he wrote:
I was very surprised when I opened your letter on behalf of the Followers of Rupert. In a book about Rupert and Alfred Bestall they said I was "found" and that about sums up my whole career as an artist.

Drawn by Alex Cubie for 'Rupert and the Orchestra' in the Adventure Series Number 13 1952.

I was born on 1 August 1911 - so in modern jargon past my shelf life as they say - but I have good eye-sight so I still lose myself drawing and painting.

I have had an enjoyable and exciting life in this Art business.

It was almost his epitaph. The following month on 6 October 1995 he died at his home at 25 Ballybroke Street, Girvan.

James Henderson, who wrote the Rupert stories, rated Alex's work highly. He commented:

'Alex was a vastly underrated Rupert illustrator. Technically he was good. How, otherwise, could he have earned his living as an animation artist in the film industry and a staff artist with the Express Group? Alex's loose, sketchy cinematic style of drawing made for rapid production. His misfortune was to succeed Alfred Bestall with whom, inevitably, he was compared by Bestall fans'.

A memorial exhibition of his work was organized by Margaret McCance at the McKechnie Institute, Girvan in 1996.

Puzzle page by Alex Cubie from the 1989 Rupert Annual. Every letter in the alphabet is represented by at least one object. Can you write down what they are?

Cover by Alex Cubie for the 1977 Rupert Annual

Cover by Alex Cubie for the 1974 Rupert Annual

Cover by Alex Cubie for the 1975 Rupert Annual

Dr Lucy Matthews

Lucy was born in Solihull. She gained a BA and PhD in Ancient History and Archaeology from the University of Birmingham. She began as an illustrator with Rupert in 1976, when she was asked to help Alfred Bestall with his work load, on the understanding that Alfred might draw the heads of some of the central characters.

Her work can, for example, be seen in 'Rupert and the Wizard', 'Rupert and the Super-Racket', 'Rupert and the Camera', 'Rupert and the Misery Moss', and 'Rupert and the Tinker's Bell'. She also wrote some of the stories, including 'Rupert and the West Wind'. She produced some of the early L-Shapes, to introduce Alfred's stories in the Annuals.

Alfred Bestall became extremely fond of her, and visited her many times. He wrote often, giving her professional advice and encouragement. Knowing that she did not take the *Daily Express* regularly, he painstakingly cut out every episode of her stories and sent them to her.

She continued drawing Rupert until moving to Cornwall in *1985,* where she now teaches art and illustrates books.

Two surrounds drawn by Lucy Matthews for stories illustrated by Alfred Bestall in the 1977 Rupert Annual

RUPERT and

As Cubie approached retirement, several young artists were allowed to try their hand at illustrating Rupert. Of them John Harrold emerged as the successor. John is a brilliant pen and ink artist, who delights in fine detail. He has now been illustrating the little bears adventures for a longer time than Mary Tourtel, and those children who were brought up on his first adventures are now mature adults.

John was born in Glasgow on 6 December 1947, and studied there at the School of Art situated in the Charles Rene Mackintosh building.

John Harrold at work in his flat in Paris, 1997

Courtesy of Cathy Hooft

John Harrold

Harrold's first job as an illustrator was on *Fun to Cook with Rupert* (drawn in 1973, published 1974). Freddie Chaplin was impressed with this and when the opportunity occurred invited him to do work for the *Daily Express*. His first story, 'Rupert and the Worried Elves', began on 14 October 1976, and in the same year he produced games pages for the annuals. He has drawn the covers and end-papers for the annuals since 1978.

Rupert and Horace Hedgehog drawn by John Harrold and coloured by Gina Hart for the 1995 Rupert Annual.

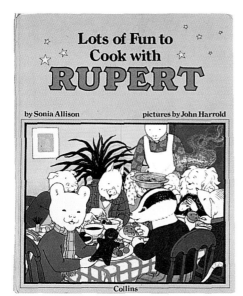

Lots of Fun to Cook with Rupert written by Sonia Allison and published by Collins in 1974.

Drawn by John Harrold and coloured by Gina Hart for the 1996 Rupert Annual.

An L-shape from 'Rupert and the Missing Snow'. Drawn by John Harrold and coloured by Doris Campbell for the 1992 Rupert Annual.

RUPERT AND THE SARDINE TOAST SCRAMBLE

Rupert and Bill Badger are at the seaside with Mr. and Mrs. Bear. One day Mr. Bear and a friend of his take them fishing. They sail their little boat into the middle of a calm bay and begin to fish. Time passes and only a few small fish are caught. Suddenly Rupert feels a tug on his line. "This must be a huge one, Bill!" he cries. Mr. Bear helps his son to heave, and soon his catch is landed. But it's not a huge fish after all - it's a large wooden crate. Inside are lots of tins of sardines. "We have caught lots of fish after all!" cries Bill. The fishing party heads for the shore. There is a photographer with a monkey who is taking pictures of the holiday-makers. "Let's get our picture taken," suggests Mr. Bear. "Mummy can hang it up when we go home." As they pose with their feet on the crate and their rods in their hand, Cap'n Barnacle rushes up. "My sardines!" he cries. "They fell overboard when I was out at sea. As a reward, let me show you how to make a special seaman's sardine snack."

YOU WILL NEED

1 cup
1 small bowl
1 fork
1 saucepan
Grill pan and rack or toaster
1 key (for opening sardines)
1 wooden spoon
4 plates
1 knife and fork for each person
4 eggs
4 teaspoons milk
Salt and pepper
2 teaspoons butter or margarine
4 slices white or brown bread
1 can sardines in oil or tomato sauce

enough for 4

Lots of Fun to Cook with Rupert written by Sonia Allison and published by Collins in 1974.

RUPERT LANDS A CATCH

What to do:

1 Break 1 egg into a cup. If it looks good and smells fresh, pour it into a small bowl. Do the same with the 3 other eggs.

2 Add milk to eggs. Sprinkle with salt and a light shake of pepper.

3 Beat with a fork until the yolks and whites are well mixed with the milk.

4 Melt the butter or margarine in a saucepan.

5 Toast the bread on both sides and keep it hot.

6 Ask a grown-up to open can of sardines.

7 Pour beaten egg into pan containing the melted butter or margarine.

8 Using wooden spoon, stir non-stop over a low heat until eggs are scrambled, thick and creamy.

9 Spread over the hot toast then stand one or two sardines on top of each.

10 Put slices of toast, with scramble and sardine topping, on to 4 plates. Eat while still hot.

Watch the birdie! Hold it there!
This snap's to show to Mrs. Bear.

19

41

RUPERT

Beppo and the Kite

Says Dr. Lion, "Why I'm here,
Is Beppo's owner's ill, I fear."

Beppo the pet monkey has always been one of Rupert's favourites, even though he is a little scamp. So Rupert is concerned when one morning he sees Dr. Lion going into Beppo's home. "Beppo's owner is not well," he tells Rupert as he hurries indoors. "Poor old lady," thinks Rupert. "Perhaps I can help by looking after Beppo for her, at least for the day. I know, I'll go and ask if I may."

"Beppo's poor mistress ill? Then he
Might be much better off with me."

"D'you think," asks Rupert, "that I may
Look after Beppo for the day?"

"That's kind of you," says the little maid who answers the door when Rupert makes his offer. "Wait here and I'll ask." When she returns she has Beppo with her. "We're very grateful," she tells Rupert. "The doctor says peace and quiet are what's needed – and that's not easy with Beppo about the place." Certainly Beppo seems happy about the arrangement and soon Rupert and he are heading for Rupert's cottage.

His owner's just too glad to let
The young bear take care of her pet.

Another outstanding L-shape by John Harrold from the 1988 Rupert Annual.

He was at first expected to draw in Bestall's later style, but was soon allowed to stamp his own personal vision on Rupert's world, blending a warm and subtle sense of humour with outstanding draughtsmanship. His line work remains unsurpassed..

John experimented with page designs, adding asymmetrical shapes to give much charm and style. He is perhaps at his best with the now famous L-shape, used to introduce the beginnings of the stories. These page lay-outs are, as works of art, as important as Bestall's endpapers.

Right: Drawn by John Harrold and coloured by Gina Hart for the 1995 Rupert Annual.

Left: Detail from a panel by John Harrold and coloured by Doris Campbell in the 1991 Rupert Annual.

Follow Rupert every day

Rupert's Memory Test

How good is your memory? Look at these frames drawn by John Harrold and coloured by Gina Hart which are portions of bigger pictures you will have seen in a story. Answer the questions below.
One clue .. *look in the 1995 Rupert Annual. page 97.*

"Courtesy of Pedigree Books Ltd."

CAN YOU REMEMBER....

1. Who is Rupert visiting?
2. Why is Rupert frightened?
3. Who has knocked Rupert over?
4. What has the professor invented?
5. What is the horse's name and to whom does it belong?
6. What are Rupert and his father trying to buy?
7. Who is Rupert running to see and why?
8. What is Captain Binnacle showing Rupert and what does it do?
9. What has Rupert got and how did he come to get it?
10. What constellation is the missing star from?
11. Who is Rupert looking for?
12. What woke Horace up?
13. Why are the pals getting a picnic?
14. Who owns the forest and why is he cross?
15. What is Rupert doing and why?
16. Who is crying and why?

John Harrold's cover for the 50th Daily Express Annual, 1985

1 Mrs. Bear, his mother.
2 Lily Duckling, a timid friend.
3 Gregory Guineapig, a young, sometimes silly, friend.
4 Dinkie, a mischievous cat.
5 Podgy Pig, a greedy but goodhearted friend.
6 Tigerlily, the Chinese Conjurer's daughter.
7 Pong-Ping who came to Nutwood from China.
8 Rich Reggie Rabbit - or is it Rex? It's one of the twins.
9 Sara, a friend from Nutwood village.
10 Pong-Ping's pet dragon, Ming.
11 Rastus, the country mouse.
12 The Gipsy Granny, an old friend.
13 Gaffer Jarge, Nutwood's oldest inhabitant.
14 The Wise Old Goat. Friendly but a bit mysterious.

15 Alfred Bestall MBE who wrote and drew the adventures of Rupert for over thirty years.
16 Margot, a little girl Rupert has known for as long as he can remember.
17 Mr. Bear, his father.
18 Billy Goat, the Wise Old Goat's nephew.
19 The Chinese Conjurer, a magician.
20 Captain Binnacle, an old seafaring friend.
21 Dr. Chimp, Nutwood's schoolmaster.
22 Beryl, one of three Nutwood Girl Guides (the others are Janet and Pauline) and owner of Dinkie.
23 Dr. Lion, Nutwood's doctor.
24 Constable Growler, village bobby.
25 An Autumn Elf. The Elves ensure that trees and growing things can rest after the summer.

26 Odmedod, a scarecrow who can talk to Rupert.
27 Jack Frost, bringer of snow and ice to Nutwood.
28 An Imp of Spring. The Imps waken everything that has slept through the winter.
29 A Nutwood Robin. When the local robins were turned yellow Rupert restored their colour for them.
30 Dutch Doll who refused to be put down the chimney with Santa Claus's other toys.
31 Chinese Doll, Rupert's guide to the Land of Games.
32 Algy Pug, a very close chum.
33 The First Rupert Annual (1936).
34 The little bear himself.
35 Bill Badger, another very close chum.
36 The Fiftieth Rupert Annual.
37 Rosalie, Podgy Pig's tiresome cousin.
38 Willie Mouse, an old firend.
39 Edward trunk, another close chum.
40 Pompey, Edward's baby brother.
41 Bingo, a brainy friend.
42 Margaret, a friend.
43 Sailor Sam, a close friend ever since they shared an Arctic adventure.
44 Beppo, a bundle of mischief.
45 Rollo, a friend, grandson of the Gipsy Granny.
46 The Old Professor, a friendly inventor.
47 The Professor's servant.
48 Ferdy Fox, usually up to no good.
49 His brother Freddy.
50 Ting-Ling, a young Chinese visitor.
51 Two of Nutwood's Scouts.
52 Santa Claus's cowboy messenger.

Saturday 5th June 1993

Ottoline was very much a joint creation between Ian Robinson and John Harrold. Ian was keen to add a female animal character to Rupert's inner circle and finally decided on an otter. John created her look, after they called her Ottoline, which was inspired by Ottoline Morrell and the Garsington set of the 1920's. Her character emerged during the writing of the first story in which she appeared and quickly became estblished as she reappeared, both in the Daily Express stories and in the Nelvana TV series.

Ottoline drawn by John Harold and after colouring by Gina Hart for the 1994 Rupert Annual.

Below: Drawn by John Harrold in the 1993 Rupert Annual.

His gifted and accomplished style has been much admired, both by children and connoisseurs. His emergence virtually coincided with the job of producing Rupert passing, in 1978, to James Henderson, Syndication Editor of *Express Newspapers*. The two made an effective team, Harrold graphically realising the other's plots in a way Henderson found quite extraordinary.

James and John's partnership lasted for over twelve years and saw the emergence of such memorable new characters as Rika, the Sage of Um and Little Yum. James writes of John: '*His impressive graphic skill apart, John has, I rapidly discovered, an almost uncanny capacity to realise in line and colour what the writer has visualised, no matter how exotic or abstruse the concept. Over*

and over again I was amazed by this quality in him. John's teeming illustrations fulfil his intention that a young reader should be able to be immersed in them, constantly finding something fresh. Just study his cover for the 50th Rupert annual in which virtually every Nutwood character appears, including Bestall himself. Masterly isn't an excessive description of it'.

While living at Ashley Court in London John found that day-time interruptions were too great. Like Bestall, he developed a semi-nocturnal routine to meet the stringent deadlines. He began to draw Rupert at 2 pm and kept going until 4 or 5 the following morning, during which time he would get 3 to 4 panels completed. Since moving to Paris in 1994, the interruptions became less and he is able to work more normal hours.

In 1990 James Henderson retired and was succeeded by Ian Robinson, the present Rupert editor. Ian had a great deal of experience writing for children's books and, to ensure continuity, worked closely with Henderson on the 1989 and 1990 annuals.

Robinson's partnership with John has been an instant success, delighting Rupert readers across the generations.

Ian Robinson rates Harrold's artwork highly: '*He combines the best of Tourtel and Bestall. He is very skilled at telling a story episode by episode - keeping a real sense of forward motion to each frame that adds to the strip-format's natural 'cliff-hangers'.*

Below: End paper by John Harrold for the 1982 Rupert Annual.

47

Gina Hart **b.1941**

Gina Hart is the current colourist for the Rupert annuals, and her work is greatly admired by both Ian Robinson and John Harrold. She was born in Bishop Stortford on 29 August 1941. Both her parents were artistic and encouraged her early talent. She studied art at the Lister College, East Ham, from the age of thirteen, her favourite subjects being landscape and figure drawing.

When she left art school three years later, she joined Amalgamated Press as a junior in the art department and gradually began work on children's productions, and later as a colourist. The company changed to Fleetway and then IPC Magazines. Among the characters she has coloured are Judge Dredd, Giles, Winnie the Pooh and Thomas the Tank Engine, and she also occasionally did the illustrations.

In 1986 she set up as a freelance artist, working for a number of companies including the *Sunday Express Magazine*.

Her first colouring job involving Rupert was for Ian Robinson on a Spot the Difference page for the 1991 annual, and she has been colouring the Rupert stories since 1993. On Doris Campbell's retirement she became main colourist.

She particularly enjoys her work with Rupert, not just because she admires John Harrold's abilities as an illustrator, but also because she delighted in Rupert as a child, read him to her son and is now reading him to her grandson.

Often she has to work to tight deadlines and on one occasion had a courier sit and watch television while he waited for her to alter a piece of artwork so that he could take it straight back.

John Harrold commented: "The Daily Express was most fortunate to find this worthy successor to Doris. Her watercolour technique is faultless, with its immaculately graded washes, and perfectly judged colouring. She comprehends exactly the aesthetic intentions of the illustrator and when colouring never interferes with the composition balance. She is a meticulous perfectionist".

Three panels coloured by Gina Hart and drawn by John Harrold for the 1995 Rupert Annual.

Handlebar plane, Codeg, 1977

Rupert on his Scooter,
Marx Toys Ltd, 1973

Silverplated money box,
Butler, 1982

Rupert Jumpers, Codeg, 1974

The Followers of
Rupert, Annual
General Meeting
Badge, 1997

Viewmaster, GAF Corp, 1976

Rupert bagatelle, Marx Toys Ltd, 1970's

Rupert Bubblebath, Euromark Ltd, 1992

Pay and Take
Giveaways, 1960's

Rupert Nightlight,
Sealedglow Nighlights, 1974

Rupert puppet.
Pelham, 1970's

Rupert and his friends - Posters to Colour by
Numbers, Whitman, 1974

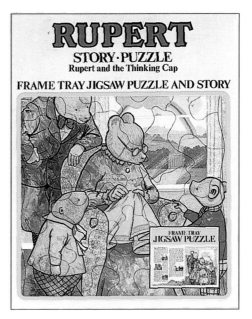

Rupert Hoop-La, Goodtime Toys, 1982

Rupert Story-Puzzle, Hope, 1976

Ruperts by
Pedigree, 1960

Rupert's Colouring Calendar published by Beaverbrook

Book of Stickers,
Introduct, 1994

Postcards,
Reflex Marketing Ltd
1992-3

Match 'A' Patch Memory Game.
Skirrid, 1980

Dumpy Alarm Clock, Brampton Clock Co, 1986

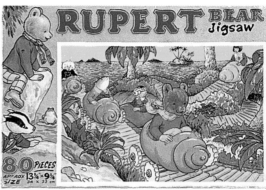

Rupert Bear Jigsaw, Hope, 1970

All the items displayed are from the collection of Peter Blackburn

Rupert Super Slate
Bell Toys, 1969

The Rupert and Friends Knitting Book,
Patons Beehive, 1991, with jumper knitted by
Sheila Blackburn,

Bendy Rupert,
Bendy Toys Ltd,
1969

RUPERT AND
THE BRIGANDS

THEY went straight to the spot whence came
  Those cries and found a Hare,
Who lay quite helpless on the ground,
  Fast captured in a snare.

Then quickly Rupert set her free.
  "Thank you, kind sir," she cried;
" Oh, if you had not passed this way
  I surely would have died."

Said Rupert: " We must get along,
  This little man and I,
Straight to the Fairy Miller's house,
  So we must say Good-bye."

From Rupert Little Bear Adventures No 2, by Mary Tourtel. Published 1924 by Sampson Low, Marston and Co, Ltd

Ralph David Blumenfeld 1864-1948

It was R.D.Blumenfeld, as editor of the *Daily Express,* who voiced concern over the growing popularity of children's strips in rival newspapers. He made the decision that the *Daily Express* would develop its own strips. He could not have envisaged the pleasure that this decision would bring to generations of children across the world.

Blumenfeld was born in America on 7 April 1864, the son of editor David Blumenfeld. He became a reporter for various journals including the Chicago Herald, and the New York Herald. He came to England, where he worked on the Daily Mail between 1900-1902. He was editor of the *Daily Express* between 1902-1932 and died on 17 July 1948.

Herbert Bird Tourtel 1874-1931

Herbert Tourtel was born in Guernsey on 7 January 1874 the son of Peter, a merchant. He was educated at Elizabeth College and at Trinity College, Cambridge. He then gained a temporary job as a tutor to the children of the Gilmour family in Glasgow, reading French, English Literature and English History. His ambition was to become a poet, and he greatly admired the work of Lord Tennyson, Thomas Gray, Shelley and Lord Byron.

He had met Mary Caldwell while she was at the Royal College of Art, when she was recommended as an illustrator for his poems. It was not long before he fell deeply in love with her.

The start of the romance is chronicled in Herbert's diary of 1898-1900 recently discovered in Australia, and now in the collection at Canterbury Heritage Museum.

November 9 Saw Miss Caldwell at S. Kensington. She is a most beautiful girl - "A daughter of the gods, divinely tall, and most divinely fair". Her illustrations to my poems are simply splendid.

November 10 Called on Lord Hamilton with drawings and Poems.

Mary Tourtel

Sunday November 13 'Met Miss Caldwell at South Kensington at 3.30... I like her very much: she is one of the most frank, interesting, candid girls I have ever met - and what is more, unlike so many of these clever girls, she is distinctly handsome'.

Wednesday November 16 Met Miss Caldwell at 3.30 at South Kensington. Came home for tea and sat in the firelight gleam until 7.30 when we dined with Meakin. Talked of everything under the sun with the freedom of thought. I have never felt the same feeling of absolute sympathy with anyone before. It was an evening to be remembered - the sort of evening which flashes back across one's consciousness when years have passed'.

Wednesday December 21. Met Portia [Herbert's nickname for Mary] at S.Kensington. I am full of hope for the future now and she does not diminish that hope.

Thursday Dec 29 Dreamt of Portia again. All the time I am awake, I think of her: Whenever I sleep I dream of her. Wrote to her this evening, a very short letter.

Saturday Dec 31 The day after tomorrow Portia will be back again... I wish I could obliterate the interval between this moment and Portia's return.

Sunday January 22 1899. What words can never convey. The day of hope realized. Our informal engagement. I am Portia's, Portia mine.

Saturday Feb 4 ..... It seems to me now more than ever, that there are two classes in the world - Portia and others, and there is none other like Portia......More than ever I feel that evermore my future is bound up with Portia.

July 30 ....I could not tear myself away from Portia and I decided to spend the holidays somewhere in Kent as near Canterbury as was possible, so I altered my labels to Canterbury and we came away together. I stayed for a week in Canterbury and there saw Portia every day. We had to be careful, for we do not desire the fact of our engagement to become vulgar property just at present.

Monday 21 August Met Portia at 10 o'clock at the old stile. We came on to the Patrixbourne farm in the hope of sketching some carthorses, but just arrived as they were going to the stables for their dinner. We came on to my rooms, had lunch, then returned and Portia sketched the horses. One man was very fond of his horses and quite in rapture with a sketch of his head which Portia made. We walked back. I had tea in Canterbury and then we met at the station and went on to Bridge. From there we walked halfway through the Park, then sat down and dreamed of the future, and how we would decorate and furnish the various rooms of our mansions. It was a most pleasant night and we smoked to keep small fowl of the night at a distance. Portia is very much afraid of grass hoppers and such small deer. We walked back into Canterbury and I caught the 9.55 home.

[*No entries occur in the diary for nearly a year, until this final entry.*]

1900 June 25 What a change in my prospects and my position since the last entry in this diary! A few days after the last entry I joined the staff of the "Weekly Sun" as junior on probation. In January I was engaged permanently. In February I was placed in partial command. In March I was given entire control as Chief of Staff under Dr Mackew as Managing editor. At 26 I find myself editing a splendid paper with a unique position and a good salary. And all through a Golden chance..

Oh, what a dreadful smash there was:
The geese came hissing round.
Two rabbits coming o'er the hill
Saw someone on the ground.

They were the Twins, Reggie and Rex.
Said Rex: "What's happening there?"
Both ran up swiftly. Reggie cried:
"It's Rupert, I declare."

Drawn by Mary Tourtel from Rupert Little Bear's Adventures Number Two, published 1924

Unfortunately, Herbert by now was probably too busy to keep up his diary. The couple married by licence on 26 September 1900 in Stoke Poges Church, presumably chosen because of their love of poetry. This was the church that inspired Thomas Gray to write his famous elegy.

Herbert's career in newspapers led him to work for the *Daily Express* as a night editor and then as a senior executive. When he had time he wrote the verses for his wife Mary's Little Bear stories.

Mary's niece, Mrs Mabel Matthews, remembered Herbert Tourtel as a short, dark, tubby man who smoked cigars and liked a drink, and was full of fun. He was the definitive jolly uncle, a great entertainer who had them in fits of laughter. Throughout his life he remained devoted to his wife.

Herbert's great passion was flying, and Mary used to say she also liked 'seeing the land as birds see it'. In some adventures this interest comes through with Rupert becoming a pilot.

When Herbert developed heart trouble, the couple moved to Italy and then to Germany, where he entered a Sanatorium at Bad Nanheim. On 6 June 1931 he died aged 57. He was cremated at Golders Green crematorium, and remained there until Mary's death when his remains were removed by the undertakers, C.W.Lyons and Son and placed with Mary's in a double sized marble urn, which was buried in St Martin's Churchyard in Canterbury.

When he began his career as an aspiring poet, he could not have envisaged that millions of people would read the verses he composed for Rupert. He has gained a wider readership than many poet laureates, and the rhymes under the stories, now a special feature of the annuals, often give children one of their first pleasurable introductions to poetry.

Stanley Marshall with Alfred Bestall, 1947

Stanley Marshall (Uncle Bill) d.1950

Born in Yorkshire. Lord Beaverbrook transferred him from his northern newspapers, where Stanley Marshall had successfully started children's clubs. He brought him to the *Daily Express* to form the immensly popular Rupert League.

He used to walk to work, and by an uncanny coincidence he sometimes chatted to a man who regularly walked in the same direction - a man called Alfred Bestall. After sending in Rupert artwork Alfred was astonished to be interviewed by his walking companion. Bestall was given the job!

Stanley's task was to approve Bestall's rough drawings and stories, making some suggestions for possible improvements. It was also his idea to collect the stories together and create the first Rupert annual. In 1936 *The New Adventures of Rupert* was published priced two shillings and sixpence. It contained five new stories and was a great success.

During the war, Stanley was in charge of the fire party, dealing with the many incendiary bombs landing on the roof of the *Daily Express* buildings.

He allowed Alfred Bestall to introduce the paper-folding exercises to the annuals. When Bestall became overworked he got in Enid Ash and Alex Cubie to help, and wrote a couple of stories, one being Rupert and the Ticking Box. He eventually died from a heart attack in 1950.

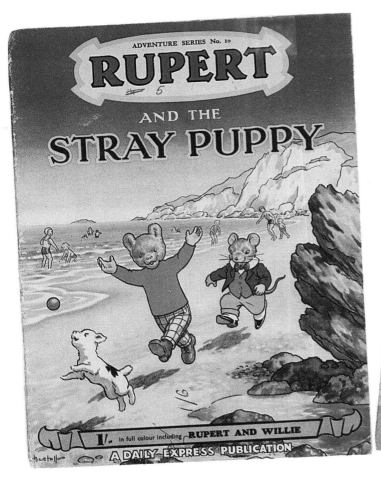

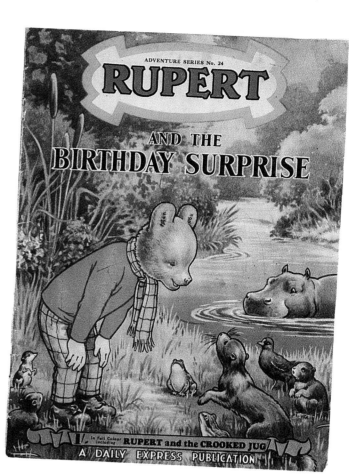

A selection from the Rupert Adventure Series published approximately quarterly by Oldbourne Book Co. Ltd from 1948

Albert Asher

Albert was responsible for a number of successful promotions including The Round Britain Yacht Race. He instigated a series of Rupert tales in quarterly book form, which became known as 'The Adventure Series'.

Frederick Chaplain **d.1981**

He succeeded Stanley Marshall as children's editor about 1950. He had great experience producing comics for young children, including work on the *Tiger Tim* comics at Amalgamated Press and on Walt Disney's *Mickey Mouse Weekly*. He also wrote Little Bonni Blue Bell in *Rainbow*.

An energetic man, he could produce the dificult rhyming couplets with great ease. However, pressure of work meant that he sometimes had to employ other writers for the task, the most successful of these was Muriel Willa. He was given the responsibility for producing the Adventure stories, and was encouraged in his work by his wife Edith, who thought very highly of the little bear.

According to Muriel Willa, Freddie was absolutely wonderful to work for, and very kind and helpful When he sent her urgent work one day he sent a telegram saying 'Rupert arriving Christchurch station 2.30 pm' He took his responsibilities seriously and was very anxious that children should not be frightened, an attitude shared by Alfred Bestall, who felt that *"Nutwood seemed to fit 'Chappie' as if he had been born there"*.

Ian Robinson believes that Freddie was able to continue the strong vein of whimsy that Bestall brought to many of his most enjoyable stories.

Edith Fraser **b.1903**

Edith was the wife of Peter Fraser, a close friend of Alfred Bestall from his student days. Like Alfred, Peter produced illustrations for *Punch* and the two men shared a studio in Whitefriars Street, London before the first world war.

Edith and her husband moved to Seasalter, near Whitstable, where they lived happily in a modest army hut, called 'Gunnavoe'. Alfred used to visit them regularly at weekends and go sailing with Peter. Their army hut was used by Alfred to base his drawings of Sailor Sam's cottage.

When Peter died Alfred found Edith work writing rhymes and captions for the annuals. She said in an interview with Paul Crampton *"Bestall was extraordinarily kind to me, and got me onto this, and said would you mind if we sent you some ideas for Rupert as we were stuck, a great rush on at the office, or something like that. I'd never done anything like this before. So I did, and I was extremely grateful, because I'd sunk without trace, and never visualised that I could work on my own, and this got me started"*.

Her favourite stories were in the 1960 annual, and she remembers writing captions for 'Rupert and the Paper Plane', 'Rupert and the Three Guides', 'Rupert and the Crystal', and couplets for 'Rupert and the Empty Cottage', 'Rupert and the Little River', 'Rupert and the Blue Star' and 'Rupert and the Windy Day'.

Sometimes her son's friends got interested in her work and chipped in with suggestions. The rhymes and captions were always wanted in a hurry. Edith was appreciated because she was able to work very quickly and meet the stiff deadlines. When Freddie Chaplain took over he found he was able to do most of his own poetry, but still employed Edith on occasions. Her last work for Rupert was in 1975. After working on Rupert she also wrote for *Sunny Stories* and produced children's books.

Gunnavoe, Seasalter, near Whitstable, the home of Enid Fraser. It was used by Alfred Bestall as the model for Sailor Sam's cottage. The building has since been demolished.

Frank Parker b.1927

Frank Parker as Books Manager had a considerable influence on the Rupert annuals. Born on 23 June 1927 at Redmile, Leicestershire, he was educated at King Edward VII Grammar School, Melton Mowbray.

He enlisted into the Royal Navy, serving two years, before being discharged in 1947 due to partial deafness. He then worked for the *Nottingham Evening Post*, quickly becoming a branch manager in Boston, Lincolnshire, where he met his wife, who worked for the local *Lincolnshire Standard*.

He later got a job as Circulation Representative with Beaverbrook Newspapers, covering a large area of the East Midlands. He moved to head office in London in 1974 and quickly was promoted to Southern Circulation Manager of the *Daily Express*.

Following the take-over of the company by Trafalgar House he found himself responsible for the company's book publishing activities. He commented: '*I had absolutely no experience of book publishing, being thrown in at the deep end with no training or guidance regarding buying paper, printing or any other aspects of the job*'. It was the start of his serious involvement with Rupert.

In taking over the department it was his instinct to modernise the format and presentation of the stories, which he considered had become 'old hat'. He was persuaded by Freddie Chaplain and his wife Edith, that this would have disastrous consequences, so he thought very carefully before making any changes.

The most dramatic change was the size of the annual, which at the time caused considerable controversy among collectors. The reason for its change was based on commercial considerations, mainly with a view to arresting falling sales. He became aware that the small size of the Rupert annual meant that it was lost when displayed amidst a host of Christmas annuals and other children's books (the majority being of A4 size or larger). After a year of fighting the issue with his Board of Directors, and with strong support from James Henderson, he was allowed to re-vamp the book.

While taking the size up, he reduced the number of pages from 120 to 96, but increased the weight of the cover-boards to compensate for the reduced bulk of the book. Initially there was a loud outcry from some ardent Rupert fans, but the overall result was a great success, and it allowed more room for John Harrold's brilliant detailing to shine through.

After four or five years, due to obtaining more favourable printing and paper costs he was able to restore an additional eight pages, increasing the pagination to 104. To celebrate the 70th Birthday edition, he decided to encase the book.

It was also his idea to produce the facsimile annuals, and he went to great lengths to make sure they were as authentic as possible. This was a difficult task as the *Daily Express* possessed none of the original artwork for this particular annual in the archives. Through advertising in a Collectors magazine he was able to locate a mint copy of the first edition. It took him some time to track down the right paper, his merchants, McNaughton Papers, scoured Europe for him. Every effort was made to match the printing quality, and he was eventually able to achieve a worthy and faithful replica of the original.

It was Frank Parker's inspiration that established John Harrold's position as official Rupert artist. John was at the time a freelance, and was producing illustrations for other companies. He could not always take on the Rupert stories, or give them the time they deserved. Frank Parker could see that John was easily the best artist for the job and suggested that he be given a contract. This allowed John to devote his time to Rupert and from that point his work blossomed.

Frank Parker retired in 1990 aged 63.

Muriel Willa b.1927

Muriel was employed as a Rupert verse writer. She was born in South Shields on 29 January 1927. Her father, Toivo, came from Karelia, a part of Finland now belonging to Russia, and her mother Edella came from Hangö, also in Finland. When she was two, the family moved to Wandsworth, where her father was a pilot on the River Thames. When he died in 1935, she and her mother moved to smaller accommodation in Southbourne, near Bournemouth, her brother being sent to relatives in Birmingham.

She remembers as a child reading one of Mary Tourtel's Rupert books: *"I have never forgotten the special mysterious feeling engendered by the illustrations and text"*.

She had her first work, a riddle, published when she was about seven, in a comic called *Bubbles,* and was rewarded by the publisher with a fountain pen. In 1946 she trained as a State Registered Nurse at Nottingham City Hospital. She took midwifery training in Edinburgh and near Bathgate, Scotland gaining a S.C.M., and undertook various nursing jobs including neurosurgical nursing, and also taught for a while in a School of Nursing, before finishing as a sister in a home for sick ex-servicemen. Eventually she had to give it up after repeated back trouble following an operation for a slipped disc in 1951.

She sent a script for a Rupert story to the *Daily Express* and received a nice reply from Freddie Chaplain, telling her that the story was 'unsuitable for present-day Rupert', but that he noticed that she had written some good couplets and would she like to try writing some verse for a Rupert story.

She was extremely good at this and could rattle them off. She wrote couplets regularly from 1962 to 1975, for both Freddie Chaplain and James Henderson . She also wrote some of the captions to go under the pictures that appeared in the *Daily Express*, including for Rupert and the Capricorn.

She made it her objective to write the couplets for an entire story without repeating the same rhymes at all, and usually succeeded. She sent Freddie Chaplain

two Rupert stories, but he decided that neither was quite right and concocted a third story combining the best ideas from each.

James Henderson considers her as one of the great 'unsung heroes' in the Rupert story. One of the stories for which she wrote the couplets was 'Rupert and the Winter Woolly', in the 1965 Rupert Annual.

"That wall may shield us from the worst!"
Cries Rupert, who recovers first.

"I'm glad this wall is strong and big,
We're quite safe here," says Podgy Pig.

"How suddenly that strong wind dropped!"
Cries Rupert, when the gale has stopped.

Verses by Muriel Willa, drawings by Alfred Bestall and colouring by Doris Campbell from the 1965 Rupert Annual.

RUPERT STOPS A FIGHT

"Wait! Here's your dragon!" Rupert cries.
Sir Claud swings round with popping eyes.

But will they fight? Before that's clear
Algy and Growler both appear.

"To hunt a dragon or to fight
Without a licence is not right!"

Then PC Growler, looking grim,
Says that the knight must come with him.

"Wait! Here's your dragon!" At Rupert's cry Sir Claud swings round and his eyes pop. The dragon nods. Silence. "Well –" Sir Claud and the dragon begin. "After you," the dragon offers. "Well, I suppose we'd best get on with the, er, combat," mumbles Sir Claud. "Must you?" Rupert asks. Sir Claud stares. "It's my job to slay this dragon!" he says. "If you do you won't have a job," argues Rupert. "Hadn't thought of that," admits Sir Claud. Just then Algy and PC Growler arrive.

"Please dismount and let me see your dragon-hunting licence!" demands Growler. Sir Claud's jaw drops. "I need no licence!" he cries, climbing down. "In Nutwood you do!" says Growler. "And since plainly you don't have one I'll have to take you in while we sort this out." "How long will that take?" demands the knight. "Couple of days," Growler reckons. And Rupert notices that, far from being upset, Sir Claud seems glad not to have to fight.

P.C.Growler demands to see Sir Claud's dragon hunting licence. Delightful whimsy from James Henderson with drawings by John Harrold and colouring by Doris Campbell from the 1989 Rupert Annual.

James Henderson
b.1925

James Henderson, a gifted writer, played an important role in Rupert's development. He steered the production of Rupert through a difficult period of transition and deserves much credit for taking Rupert into a new era. Together with Frank Parker, he was responsible for enlarging the page size of the Rupert books, adopting standard EEC book formats.

James was born in Edinburgh on 24 March 1925, the son of Mary Burgoyne Yorke and John Henderson, who was described on James's birth certificate as a carpet buyer ('*He certainly knew a lot about exotic carpets, especially the Levantine and Near Eastern kinds, sought by collectors*'). James was raised in what he describes as '*the genteel Morningside district of the city*,' which he feels prepared him for the '*culture shock of Nutwood*'.

He began as a trainee-reporter with the Scottish division of the mighty Kemsley newspaper chain, which began an association with the Fourth Estate which was to span nearly half a century. James writes:

'*Had anyone hinted that it would culminate with me as our man in Nutwood I'd have urged them to try taking*

How much is boy and how much is bear?

The physical ambiguity of Rupert has been of considerable amusement to James Henderson.

Where does the skin stop and the fur start? The problem inspired him to write the following verse

Rupert, when his tummy aches,
His problem to a doctor takes.
But when he has le mal de tête,
His people take him to a vet.

more water with the stuff since it was plainly getting to their brain. As far as I was concerned Rupert was a kids' feature in a rival sheet which inexplicably occupied valuable column inches on, of all places, their leader page at a time when tabloids were restricted to eight pages and broadsheets to four. I've been told that the Express's then proprietor, Lord Beaverbrook, saw Rupert as a morale-booster'.

However, his career was interrupted when he volunteered for the Fleet Air Arm. After de-mob he graduated from hard newspaper reporting to feature-writing and a half-page show-biz feature in one of the Sunday tabloids. He then took a reporter's job in Nairobi for a couple of years, before coming home to become a sub-editor on the Central desk of Reuters, handling hard news from overseas correspondents.

In 1952 the Mau Mau emergency in Kenya was making international headlines and London Express News and Features Service, the syndication division of Beaverbrook Newspapers was looking for someone with a 'Kenya' background. So on the 11 November he joined the *Daily Express*, where he was to remain for the rest of his working life.

Within a couple of years he was promoted to syndication editor, and started doing Rupert by chance. In James's own words:

'*Among the features we syndicated was Rupert, but since this demanded no editorial intervention the process was virtually automatic and my association with Nutwood*

Let's call it Terry, if we may
Its proper name is hard to say

Terry the pterodactyl from a story written by James Henderson, drawn by John Harrold and coloured by Doris Campbell in the 1988 Rupert Annual.

The Sage of Um, one of James Henderson's creations, takes Rupert in his flying umbrella
in the cover art work by John Harrold for the 1988 Rupert Annual

was at best tenuous. Until..... until....

Until the fateful day that someone hustled into my room, landed a great wodge of paper on my desk with the dreaded preamble "There! Be a good chap..." and went onto say that they were having a crisis in the Books department, because the estimable Freddie Chaplain (I use the adjective sincerely), the Rupert editor, was too ill to cope with the proofs of the forthcoming Rupert annual, and would I spare a moment (get the wording!) to have a look. Remember, I was Rupert illiterate, I'd seen neither the original text, nor the artwork. But knowing Freddie Chaplain's professional reputation and that he'd been in charge up to this point I nodded it through and the Books Department breathed again.

Little did I realise the enormity of what I'd done. The impression was now established that I knew something about Rupert so that when it became clear that Freddie wasn't going to be able to take up the reins again they were pressed into my untutored hands. It was typical of Freddie Chaplain that, seriously ill as he was, he rode to the rescue, invited me to his home and briefed me in detail on how to cope with Rupert.'

Henderson developed his natural talent for children's story writing, and was cleverly able to weave in his wry sense of humour. He hated doing the rhymes, which he found time consuming and he constantly used a rhyming dictionary, which never worked - but he referred to it anyway.!

He retired on his 65th birthday on 24 March 1990, after working jointly for a brief hand-over period with Ian Robinson.

Ian commented: *"James paid Rupert the compliment of taking children's stories very seriously. He always insisted on logical plots and strong continuity, basically 'playing fair' with the readers. He was able to add to Rupert's world in a way that kept it fresh and prevented an over-reverent 'heritage' approach creeping in. Examples of his best creations are Sage of Um, Sir Humphrey Pumphrey and Rika. On a personal level, he taught me a great deal about writing episodic stories for daily publication. We worked closely together for just over a year, which allowed me to learn on the job rather than being thrown into the deep end."*

Ian Robinson b.1957

Ian is the current Rupert Editor. He was born in Watford on 9 July 1957, the son of a company manager. His mother was a school teacher. He went to school in Bournemouth and university at Warwick, where he studied history and politics.

His first job was as a copywriter with Macmillan Education, which was good training for writing precise copy to deadlines. He moved into Macmillan's editorial offices in London and worked on their adult/trade list for about five years before becoming a freelance writer.

His first published books were stories for children, jointly illustrated by his wife Gill (whom he married in 1978) and her father Ronald Embleton.. They included *The Magic Lake, The Magic Forest, The Magic Mountain* and *The Magic Castle*. These books helped Ian get the Rupert editor job when it became available, although he still had to sit an 'exam' in writing rhyming couplets.

Ian joined the *Daily Express* in 1989 working in the books department as an Assistant Editor. At first, he helped to produce the Rupert Annual and gradually

"Well done!" laughs Watson. "Clever you!"
It's just what Sherlock Holmes would do!"

Rupert on the trail of a thief at the British Museum from a story written by Ian Robinson, drawn by John Harrold and coloured by Gina Hart in the 1995 Rupert Annual.

"Hello!" calls Rupert eagerly.
"We're off to buy a Christmas tree!"

But when they reach the shop, the pair
Soon learn that there are no trees there!

"I'm sorry! They're in short supply.
The forest's sick. I don't know why!"

began writing stories with James Henderson, who was due to retire. Their first joint story, published in 1989, was Rupert and the Runaway Balloon, although James wrote the final version that appeared in the *Daily Express*. Other joint stories were 'Sparklers', 'Stolen Snowmen', 'Golden Apples' and 'Gardens Mystery'.

Ian, an accomplished children's writer, has gone on to produce some first rate stories - as fine as anything written in the long history of Rupert. He also played an important advisory role in the popular Nelvana television series of Rupert's adventures.

Ian, a very modest and kindhearted man, is secure in his own ability, and he is openly able to encourage John Harrold to contribute ideas to the stories. This flexible approach has brought the very best out of both of them.

The process normally works as follows. Ian conceives the story and breaks it down into episodes. John Harrold then adds and embellishes the story and begins the panels in consultation with Ian. This is accomplished by fax and phone. When the panels are eventually completed Ian writes the final text and last of all he produces the verses.

Ian's selection of Gina Hart as the colourist to succeed Doris Campbell has ensured that a first-rate team is continuing the enchanting world of Rupert bear.

It is a snowy December morning and Rupert and Mr. Bear are on their way to buy a Christmas tree. As they walk along the High Street, Rupert spots some of his chums, peering in the window of the toy shop. "Hello!" calls Bill. "Not long to wait for Christmas now!" When they reach the greengrocer's Mr. Bear stops with a gasp. "Dear me!" he cries. "They haven't got a single tree left! Let's go in and see what's wrong . .

"Sorry!" says Mr. Chimp. "I normally order lots of trees for Christmas, but this year there just aren't any to be found. Something's wrong with the forest and none of the pine or spruce are good enough to use!" "What a shame!" says Rupert. "It won't be the same without a tree . . ."

Three panels from Ian Robinson's story 'Rupert and the Christmas Tree' illustrated by John Harrold and coloured by Gina Hart from the 1995 Rupert Annual.

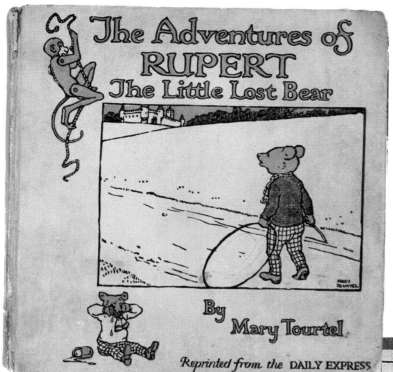

The Adventures of The Little Lost
Bear by Mary Tourtel, published
in 1921 by Nelson.
The first Rupert Book.

The Rupert Little Bear's Adventure Number One by
Mary Tourtel. Published by Sampson Low, Marston
and Co, Ltd in 1924. It was the first Rupert book to
have a full colour cover.

The New Adventures of Rupert published in 1936 by
Greycaines. The first Rupert annual and featuring
stories by Alfred Bestall. The verses were revived to run
under each picture. This format was the inspiration of
Stanley Marshall. It was an enormous success.

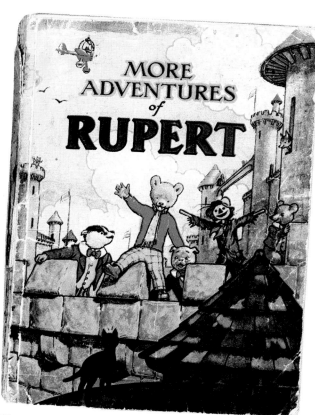

Rupert's Adventure Book 1940, published by Greycaines. The first Rupert annual featuring stories by Alfred Bestall in colour.

More Adventures of Rupert, 1942 published by Harrison. The first annual to appear in paperback.

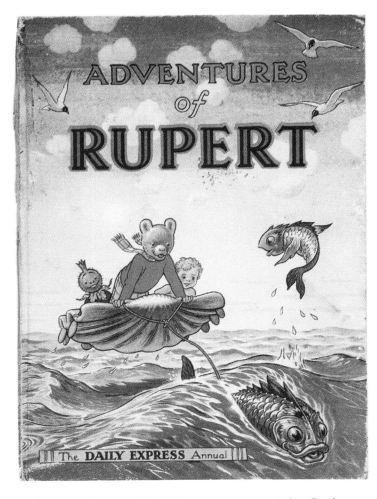

Adventures of Rupert, 1950. The annual returns to hardback.

1973 Rupert Annual - Alfred Bestall's last annual cover. The tradition of the brown faced Rupert on the cover of the annuals was broken without consultation. Alfred was upset at having his careful artwork ruined. He would have never set a white head against a white sky, and the alterations made a nonsense of his careful use of light and shade. Reportedly three examples of the original brown faced cover exist, produced in an effort to appease the artist. They are the envy of all Rupert collectors.

1974 Rupert Annual. Alex Cubie's first cover.

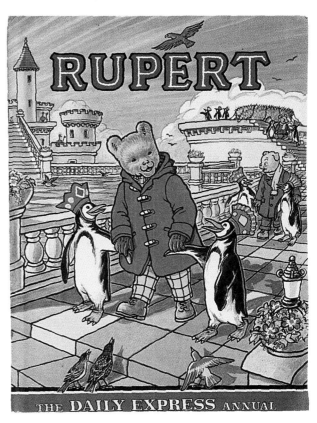

1977 Rupert Annual. Alex Cubie's last cover.

Rupert Annual 1978. John Harrold's first cover.

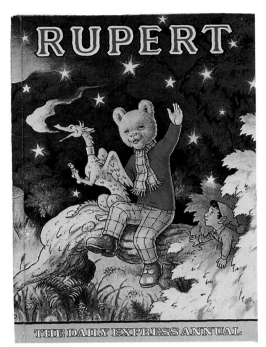

*Rupert Annual 1979.
The last of the smaller format annuals.*

Rupert Annual 1980 drawn by John Harrold. It was the first of the larger format annuals.

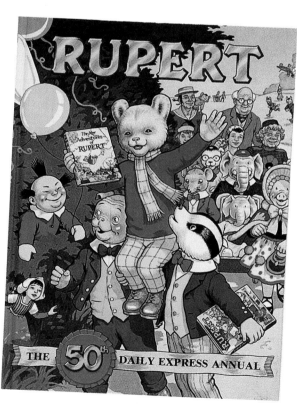

Rupert Annual 1985 - The 50th Daily Express Annual. Drawn by John Harrold it features all of Rupert's main chums and on the back includes a portrait of Alfred Bestall. James Henderson described it as a masterpiece.

1993 Rupert Annual - cover by John Harrold. The first contribution of colouring by Gina Hart, who assists Doris Campbell with some of the stories.

1991 Rupert Annual - cover by John Harrold. The first time Ian Robinson contributes and the last annual under the direction of James Henderson.

1994 Rupert Annual - cover by John Harrold. The last time Doris Campbell contributes colour work to the stories.

1995 Rupert Annual - cover by John Harrold marking the 75th Anniversary of Rupert Bear. The stories are all from the current team of writer Ian Robinson, artist John Harrold and colourist Gina Hart.

RUPERT AND DREAMLAND

"The surreal atmosphere and magic that Mary Tourtel brought to Rupert sets the tone for all the stories that followed"
Ian Robinson - Rupert editor

Courtesy of Chris Beetles Gallery, London

Rupert hides behind the Wise Old Goat in a drawing by Mary Tourtel, 1922.

Three panels drawn by Alfred Bestall

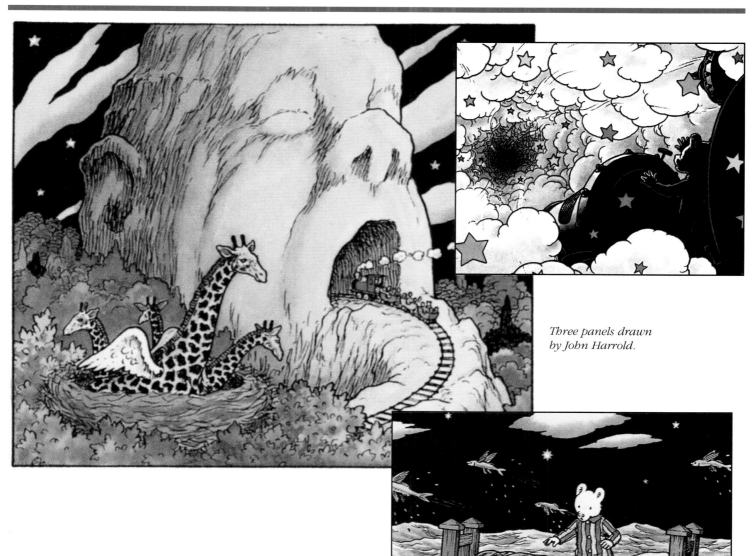

Three panels drawn
by John Harrold.

"Rupert is pure enjoyment"
commented Lord Rogers, the
architect who credits Rupert
as an influence on his much
acclaimed Pompidou Centre
in Paris. The Rupert
illustration is from 'Rupert'
Elfin Bell' (1948) by Alfred
Bestall from the 1951 Rupert
Annual.

John Harrold writes: "Rupert is unlike other long narrative cartoon strips, in the respect that Rupert now has to appear in every frame, even if sometimes his presence is vestigial. This can pose a problem, when he is simply a passive observer of an otherwise animated scene. One has to integrate him in a way which neither overburdens the composition nor lessons the impact of the scene he is witnessing. I suspect, however, that this obligatory inclusion of Rupert contributes greatly to the appeal of the tales, since as a consequence we experience everything through his eyes."
A frame drawn by John Harrold and coloured by Gina Hart from the 1994 Rupert Annual.

Rupert is incredibly hard to draw, particularly his head. He has no eyebrows, so getting the right expression is no easy task and much of the emotion has to be achieved by body language. John Harrold is a master of this, as is shown in a frame from the 1996 Rupert Annual, coloured by Gina Hart

RUPERT BY THE SEA

Drawn by Mary Tourtel from Rupert Little Bear's Adventures Number Three published in 1925.

Drawn by Alfred Bestall and coloured by Doris Campbell from the 1960 Rupert Annual

Drawn by John Harrold and coloured by Gina Hart from the 1995 Rupert Annual

RUPERT AND THE LAW

Drawn by Mary Tourtel from Rupert Little Bear's Adventures Number Three published in 1925.

Drawn by Alfred Bestall and coloured by Doris Campbell from the 1958 Rupert Annual.

Drawn by John Harrold and coloured by Gina Hart from the 1995 Rupert Annual.

RUPERT AND ROBBERS

RUPERT AND DRAGONS

Drawn by Mary Tourtel from Rupert Little Bear's Adventures Number Two published in 1924.

Drawn by Mary Tourtel from Rupert Little Bear's Adventures Number Three published in 1925.

Drawn by Alfred Bestall from the 1942 Rupert Annual

Drawn by Alfred Bestall and coloured by Doris Campbell from the 1954 Rupert Annual.

Drawn by John Harrold and coloured by Gina Hart from the 1996 Rupert Annual

Drawn by John Harrold and coloured by Doris Campbell from the 1989 Rupert Annual.

Rupert goes Dutch

Rupert is known as Bruintje Beer (Little Brown Bear) in Holland. In the 1920's the Dutch national newspaper *Algemeen Handelsblad* decided to negotiate with the *Daily Express* for the bear's appearance. Much haggling occurred with the Dutch asking for a reduction because Herbert Tourtel's rhymes would not easily translate directly into Dutch.

Met Wim Das uit Pick-nicken

· De dag, nadat Bruin Beer weer in de stad gekomen is, — hij was met zijn Moeder naar het strand geweest — klopt iemand aan de deur. Wie kan dat zijn, denkt Bruin Beer.
· Hij gaat kijken en tot zijn grote vreugde ziet hij dat het Wim Das, zijn liefste vriendje, is.
„Zeg Bruin vraag je Moeder of je met mij en de tweeling Ko en Nijn naar het bos mag gaan pick-nicken. Zou ze het goed vinden?"

Above: Rupert's debut in Holland as Bruintje Beer on 5 November 1929.
Below: Another of Mary Tourtel's stories translated into Dutch.

No. 51. — De Wijze Geit roeit zoo vlug ze kan, om buiten het bereik te komen van den grooten man. Weer klinkt trompetgeschal. „O, roei toch vlugger," smeekt Bruintje Beer, „kijk, daar komt hij al."
En ja, daar zien ze den Zeemijnheer. Angstig grijpt Bruintje het meisje vast. Wat zal haar lot nu weer zijn? Ze is nog zoo klein, die lieve meid. Maar daar roept opeens de Geit:

„Abra-cada-bra-hocus-
pocus-pilatus-pas!"

Heel langzaam zegt ze dat, de Wijze Geit en men ziet het, haar angst is groot. Angstig zitten allen te wachten in de boot.

Eventually a fee of £125 for six months was agreed and Bruintje Beer was able to make his Dutch début on 5 November 1929 appearing in a special children's section of the paper. The first story 'Met Wim Das uit Pick-nicken' (a re-print of Mary Toutel's 'Bill Badger's Picnic), did not rhyme, but by the second story, which started on 3 December 1929, the translators had got the hang of the difficult task.

Bruintje Beer also appeared in three other Dutch papers, all regional papers from the north - *Nieuwsblad van het Noorden*, *Leeuwarder Nieuwsblad*, and *Nieuwsblad van Friesland*. They were the same sequence of stories that had been in the national paper.

The frames for the stories were usually sent well in advance, but sometimes there was a problem and the artwork didn't get through in time. At this point the newspaper's illustrators drew their own Bruintje Beer to fill in the gaps.

In June 1931 a desperate situation developed. A section of the story 'Bruintje Beer en de toverspeelgoedmaker' (Rupert and the Magic toy maker) either hadn't arrived or hadn't been translated. The next day he was portrayed as a photograph of Rupert wrapped in bandages. According to the editors, Bruintje had fallen badly and this

Bruintje Beer 1970

was the result. The following day he also appeared in photograph form and still wrapped in bandages - this time sitting in a chair . The editors reported that he was getting better and, according to the doctor, would be back the following day. Indeed on June 11 the story continues with episode 31 as if no injury had ever occurred!

Despite such problems Bruintje Beer was a popular edition to the paper. A competition was held by the paper in 1931 for a poem to accompany Bruintje Beer that could be turned into a song. It was so well subscribed that it took the paper a week longer than planned to judge the contest.

The first Bruintje Beer books appeared in 1930, and the newspaper also produced Bruintje Beer scrapbooks, so that children could stick in the daily stories from the newspaper.

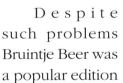

BRUINTJE BEER

6 IN 10-KLEURENDRUK UITGEVOERDE PRENTBRIEFKAARTEN VAN
BRUINTJE BEER
DE HELD UIT HET DAGELIJKSCH
KINDERVERHAAL IN HET
HANDELSBLAD _____

_____

_____

Serie I   F 0.35

The paper began using the little bear in advertising campaigns to attract new subscribers, and merchandise was adorned with his image, always under strict regulation and supervision from the staff of the newspaper. By 1934 he was registered with a Dutch Brand Registration Bureau and one publisher reproduced him without permission and got an abrupt letter demanding compensation of 250 guilders. Products being sold included Bruintje Beer post cards, games, clocks, crockery, stationery, sweets, chocolate bars, biscuits, puzzles and calendars. Many of these items are particularly prized among British collectors.

In Musselkanaal the Branbergen Biscuit factory adopted him as their logo. He appeared on packaging, biscuit and trucks between 1931-1983, and commemorative biscuits with his image were revived again in 1994 to co-incide with the Teylers Museum's Bruintje Beer exhibition.

Like his British counterpart, Bruintje Beer soon felt the call of the theatre. A musical was written and its first performance by the company 'Nederlandsch Tooneel voor Kinderen' took place at the famous Carré theatre in Amsterdam. The reviews were full of praise - both old and young felt like a child claimed the press. The Bruintje Beer Marching song from the play became a great hit and after the success in Amsterdam the company toured the country. Everywhere they went sold out. A second musical was quickly produced and 'for continuity' the same marching song remained, but a new story, sets and costumes were adopted.

During the war years there were the obvious problems with stories getting through. The paper re-printed old stories, and even re-worked Mary's drawings into new stories.

They also employed their own writers and artists, including the Amsterdam illustrator and art teacher, C.B. (Krelis) Teeuwisse (1911-1986). Teeuwisse's first illustration of Bruintje Beer was published on 1 July 1941. He completed two stories for the paper, signing with a 'T'.

In 1945 Bruintje Beer continued with Alfred Bestall's stories, but there was pressure from the Dutch government to reduce foreign obligations and in 1947 the paper announced that Bruintje's holiday was coming to an end, he was going to school and would have no more adventures.

After just one year Bruintje was back. His return was announced on the front page. Accordingly Rupert had gone to school, but he was now on holiday so that more adventures could be published. However, it seems that Bestall's stories were for some reason not as popular with the Dutch as Mary Tourtel's. On 17 August 1950 the paper once again stopped Bruintje, but this time they were more cautious giving a statement in Dutch to the effect: *'For now this is Bruintje's last adventure. His holiday is over and he has to go back to school. But maybe one day he will be back'.* And sure enough in 1959 he made another appearance, this time lasting until 1961 and again between 1972/3-1974.

From 1966 until 1972 Bruintje featured in the Dutch newspaper, *De Tijd*, first as Robbie Beer, but by the end of 1969 he had his old name of Bruintje back. From 1987-1990 he again re-appears, this time in *Donald Duck Magazine*, as a

Dutch artists used to 'doctor' Mary Tourtel's artwork for new adventures. On the right panel the shape of Bill Badger's snout can still be seen in the Wise Old Goat's cloak.

strip cartoon with speech balloons. Both Mary Tourtel and Alfred Bestall stories were used, which were rejigged. These were popular with children, but the publishers were reportedly getting large numbers of subscriptions from old people's homes. After all Bruintje Beer had been going in Holland since 1929!

He also appeared on Dutch television when NOS (the Dutch equivalent of the BBC) showed thirteen episodes of Bruintje Beer. It was the series bought from the BBC with translations by Simone Kramer.

Finally a commemorative exhibition entitled Bruintje Beer was held by the prestigious Teylers Museum in Haarlem in 1994. The museum staff expected the show to be popular, but were still taken aback by how much Bruintje was still able to capture the hearts of the Dutch nation.

Above: Bruintje Beer with speech bubbles from Donald Duck Magazine.

Right: The advertising leaflet for the Teylers Museum Bruintje Beer exhibition of 1994.

Below: A Bruintje Beer advertisement and book.

Sir Paul McCartney's BAFTA award winning video Rupert and the Frog Song was released in December 1984. The animation was by Grand Slam and the film was directed by Geoffrey Dunbar. It quickly became the second most successful video ever, only being outsold by Michael Jackson.

Paul and Linda McCartney and family visit Alfred Bestall at his cottage at Beddgelert in North Wales. Other celebrities to visit him there included actor Terence Stamp and Terry Jones of Monty Python fame.

To accompany it the song *We all Stand Together* was released and rose to number three in the charts. It was arranged by former Beatles A & R man, George Martin.

It was Alfred Bestall's endpaper from the 1958 Rupert Annual that inspired Paul McCartney to produce the record and the video. He wondered what it was the frogs were playing in the picture and decided to compose a suitable piece. Alfred Bestall was delighted and thought it "frightfully clever".

At the age of ninety-one Alfred Bestall explained to the Followers of Rupert that Paul McCartney's Frog Song should be played loudly to have full effect, because he was impressed when he heard it played that way in the recording studio.

the Frog Song

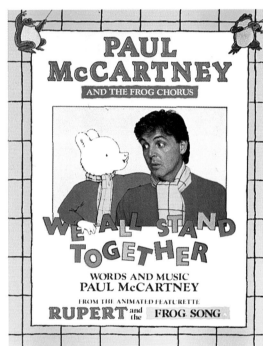

A Message from Sir Paul McCartney

For the British, Rupert is an institution - like the Queen. Britain just wouldn't be the same without him.

As a boy I always turned to the Rupert column in my parents' Daily Express and was particularly fond of the Rupert Christmas annuals. I rediscovered him in the seventies when I started reading bedtime stories to our eldest daughter Heather.

I think of Rupert as an eleven-year-old boy - I don't know why. I've got a little phrase that I associate with him: "It can be done!". I feel that is always his attitude. He is very positive and has that spark of optimism combined with a certain innocence which makes it great to set horrors and dangers against him.

Paul McCartney

RUPERT AND TRAINS

*Drawn by Mary Tourtel from Rupert Little Bear's Adventures
Number Two published in 1924.*

*Drawn by Alfred Bestall and coloured by Doris Campbell from
the 1954 Rupert Annual*

*Drawn by John Harrold and coloured by Gina Hart
from the 1996 Rupert Annual.*

RUPERT GOES TO BED

*Drawn by Mary Tourtel from Rupert Little Bear's Adventures
Number Three published in 1925.*

*Drawn by Alfred Bestall and coloured by Doris Campbell
from the 1967 Rupert Annual*

*Drawn by John Harrold and coloured by Gina Hart
from the 1996 Rupert Annual.*

1874
7 January Herbert Bird Tourtel born in Guernsey.
28 January Mary Caldwell born 52 Palace Street, Canterbury

1892
14 December Alfred Bestall born Mandalay, Burma

1900
26 September Herbert Bird Tourtel and Mary Caldwell marry at Stoke Poges, Church.

1903
President Teddy Roosevelt gives his name to the cuddly toy.
Edith Fraser, verse writer, is born.

1911
1 August Alex Cubie born at Renfrew
C.B. (Krelis) Teeuwisse, the Dutch Rupert illustrator born

1915
April The mouse Teddy Tail launched in the *Daily Mail*. Drawn by Charles Folkard.

1919
February 18 Launch of Uncle Oojah in *The Sketch* written by Flo Lancaster and illustrated by Thomas Maybank
Launch of Pip and Squeak (later to be joined by Wilfred) in the *Daily Mirror* written by Uncle Dick (Bertram J.Lamb) and drawn by Austin B.Payne

These photographs of Mary Caldwell and her family were discovered by Chris Laming in a house clearance at 11 Cromwell Road, Canterbury in 1994. Knowing the house was once owned by Mary's brother, Sam Caldwell, he decided to have some old glass negatives from the house printed up for identification.

1920

November 8 Rupert makes his first appearance in the *Daily Express*

The same year sees the Marconi Company open the first British public broadcasting s t a t i o n, gramophone discs are electrically recorded for the first time and the first automatic telephone is introduced into England.

1921

The first Rupert book entitled *The Adventures of Rupert the Little Lost Bear* published by Thomas Nelson Publication of the Little Bear Embroidery Card - thought to be the first piece of Rupert merchandising

1923

Rupert's Revenge - at the Children's Theatre, *Daily Express* Woman's Exhibition at Olympia. It was the first stage show featuring the little bear, and proceeds went to the Royal Free Hospital

1924

Sampson Low begin publishing the first of the *Rupert Little Bear's Adventures*.

1925

First of the *Rupert Little Bear Series* published by Sampson Low, Marston and Co.

1926

Mary and Herbert Tourtel staying at 36 Via Montebello, Florence.
14 October *Winnie-the-Pooh* first published

1927

January 2 The Wilfredian League of Gugnuncs formed by the *Daily Mirror* - with the pass word "Ick!Ick!Pah!Boo!"

Daily Express, 8 November 1920

Rupert Little Bear's Adventures Number Three, 1925

*Rupert Little Bear's Adventures
Number Three, 1925*

*Rupert Little Bear's Adventures
Number Two, 1924*

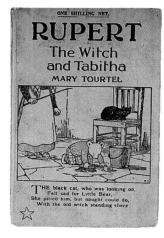

Rupert Little Bear Library, 1933

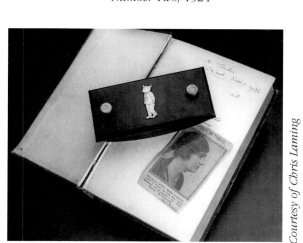

Mary Tourtel's personal blotter

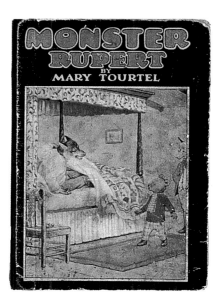

1931

1932

Colour inserts by Mary Tourtel

1928

The wise Old Goat voted the most popular character

June First of the popular yellow *Rupert Little Bear Library* series published by Sampson Low, Marston and Co.

1929

5 November Rupert's first appearance in Holland. Entitled Bruintje Beer he appears in the newspaper *Algemeen Handelsblad*

1930

The Daily Express Children's Annual started

First Bruintje Beer books appear in Holland

1931

6 June Herbert Bird Tourtel dies in Germany aged 57

First of the *Monster Rupert Books* published by Sampson Low

1932

December The *Daily Express* Rupert League formed by Stanley Marshall.

1935

June 27 Mary Tourtel's last story 'Rupert and Bill's Seaside Holiday' ended. She retires from drawing Rupert. Alfred Bestall employed.

June 28 Alfred Bestall's first story, Rupert, Algy and the Smugglers, begins in the *Daily Express*

1936

The New Adventures of Rupert published price 2/6d. This is the first real Rupert annual and was the idea of Stanley Marshall. It contained five complete stories and was printed by Greycaines.

1940

Full colour reproduction was introduced into the annuals for the first time. Entitled Rupert's Adventure Book it was printed by Greycaines and sold at 3 shillings.

1941

29 August Colourist Gina Hart born.

1942

The annual produced as a paperback with colour cover.

1945

Doris Campbell starts colouring the Rupert stories.

1947

6 December John Harrold born in Glasgow.

Anxious parents wrote to *the Daily Express* complaining that Rupert and Bingo were setting the children a bad example when handling fireworks in the story 'Rupert and the Big Bang'. Rupert got a ticking off at the end of the story.

1948

15 March Mary Tourtel dies at Canterbury Hospital aged 74. Bestall starts to sign frames of his work in full.

September The first of the *Rupert Adventure Series* published by Oldbourne Book Company Ltd. They were issued approximately quarterly in card wraps.

1949

Rupert's Famous Yellow Library large format published by Sampson Low.

1950

Rupert Annual returns to hardback cover and start of the colour endpapers.
Stanley Marshall dies.

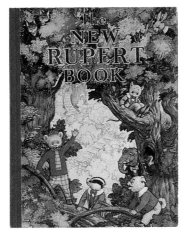

1938 Rupert Annual

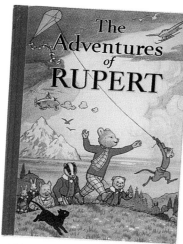

1939 Rupert Annual

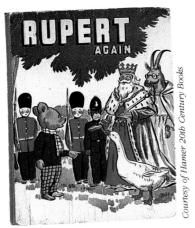

1940

Courtesy of Hamer 20th Century Books

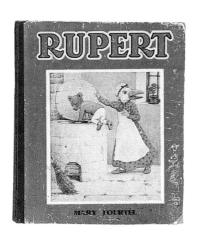

Circa 1946

Mary and Herbert Tourtel's tombstone at St Martins Church, Canterbury

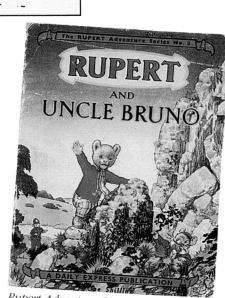

Rupert Adventure Series, 1949

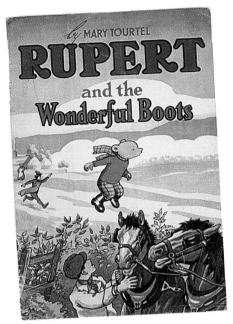

1946

1950.   *Courtesy of Hamer 20th Century Books*

Endpaper, 1958 Rupert Annual

Nestle Chocolate Bars, 1975

1979

1954

The New Rupert Colour Story Book first published.

1956

Alfred Bestall buys Penlan, Beddgelert, North Wales where he had spent much time walking with his friend Harry Adams.

1957

9 July Rupert writer Ian Robinson born in Watford.

1958

The first annual to be dated on the inside page. Bestall's famous Frog Chorus published in the annual. It later inspired Paul McCartney to write his hit song, when he wondered what they were playing.

1960

Teddy Tail ends in the *Daily Mail.*

1963

June The 50th and last in the 'Rupert Adventure Series' published.

1965

Alfred Bestall finally stops drawing the daily Rupert for the *Daily Express*. His last published story was Rupert and the Winkybickies, which ended on 22 July. He still contributed some artwork to the stories until 1982.

1970

28 October First episode of an animated puppet version of Rupert appears on ITV London region. The series continued for seven years. It was also seen in Finland, New Zealand, Portugal, The Lebanon, Hong Kong, Kenya, Jamaica, Iran, Zambia, Abu Dhabi, Malaysia, Singapore, the Ivory Coast, Malta, Algeria and Sierra Leone.

A Rupert single written by Beadle and Roker is a hit.

1946 Rupert Annual

1956

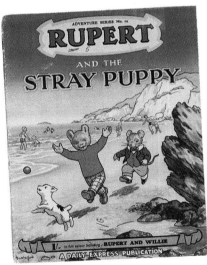
Rupert Adventure Series, 1951

Rupert Adventure Series, 1955

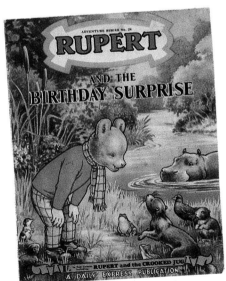
Rupert Adventure Series, 1955

1964 Rupert Annual

*The Monster
Rupert, 1949*

1969 Rupert Annual

1975 Rupert Annual

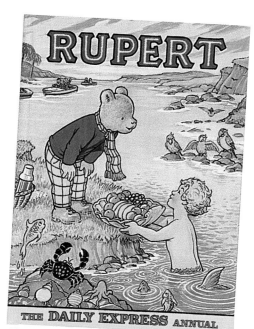

1974 Rupert Annual

1975 Rupert Annual

1971

2 January Jackie Lee releases the hit record 'Rupert' which remains in the charts for 17 weeks.

The infamous OZ trials. Charges were brought in May with the trial over July and August. The evidence included a drawing of Rupert in a state of amorous arousal!

1972

July Rupert's stage show appears at the Victoria Palace, London, before undertaking a lengthy tour of the provinces.

Release of Rupert Sings an Hour of Nursery Rhymes, produced and arranged by Barry Ainsworth and David Cullen.

1973

Alfred Bestall's last cover, which was doctored to give Rupert a white face. Alfred was so upset only three proof versions with the original brown head were printed. Sampson Low, Marston and Co Ltd publish a series of 18 *Rupert Little Bear Library* books only available at Woolworths.

1974

15 June Rupert first appears in the children's comic *Pippin* - another collectors' item. Alex Cubie's first cover and end-paper for the annuals.

Fun to Cook with Rupert by Sonia Allison and illustrated by John Harrold published by Collins.

1975

Edith Fraser and Muriel Willa retire from writing rhymes.

September 20 *Pippin* changes its name to *Pippin in Playland*.

Rupert's Christmas Carols, 4 TV Playbooks, and *6 TV Storybooks* published by Michael Stanfield Holdings Ltd.

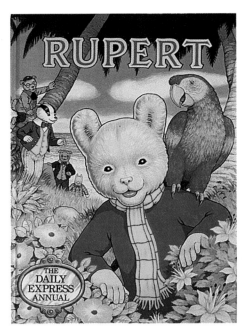

1987 Rupert Annual

1985

"*Rupert is a quiet corner of British genius*"
George Perry

"*As a child, the world of Alfred Bestall's Rupert Bear books often seemed more real to me than the real world did. It was certainly a world I wanted to inhabit: kind, secure and yet exciting. Rupert has many chums and you feel there is a lot of goodness in the air.*"
Terry Jones

1988 Rupert Annual

Alfred Bestall with Paul Crampton at the first official meeting of The Followers of Rupert, 15 September 1984

The question of Mr Bear's occupation gave rise to a series of letters that dominated the Guardian in December 1985. Suggestions included bee-keeper, gardener and publican. Other proposals included purser, mercer, college bursar and Royal Shakespeare play rehearser - but this was mainly because they rhymed. David Leathard of Sheffield noticed a 'Mr Bear' as recording engineer on a number of EMI classical recordings, and his theory was strengthened by the observation that these recordings were all made between March and June - the off-peak season for sweeping leaves.

1976

August First of 12 stories in the *Rupert Colour Library* published by Purnell**.**

14 October 'Rupert and the Worried Elves' written by James Henderson and illustrated by John Harrold begins in the *Daily Express*. It is the first time John's artwork is used for a story in the newspaper..

1977

24 January *Daily Express* goes tabloid.

Alex Cubie's last annual cover.

First of *The St Michael Book of Rupert Favourites* published.

Rupert badges sold to members and friends of the Police Federation in aid of police victims of terrorist activity in Northern Ireland, and their widows and mothers. The design of the badges changes each year.

1978

Freddie Chaplain retires.

James Henderson appointed syndication editor.

John Harrold's first cover and end-papers.

Rupert appears at the Alfred Beck Centre, Hayes Middlesex described as 'Television's Rupert Bear'.

1979

Last of the smaller format Rupert annuals.

First of the *Rupert Holiday Specials,* published by Polystyle Publications.

1980

Larger format Rupert annual introduced.

Alfred Bestall visits Mary Tourtel's grave.

Rupert's golden jubilee.

1981

Freddie Chaplain dies.

April 12 Rupert appears in The *Sunday Express Magazine*.

November 13 Last appearance of Rupert in *Pippin in Playland*.

An article on Rupert appears in the *Blue Peter Annual*.

St Michael's Adventures of Rupert published.

1982

Last contribution of artwork by Alfred Bestall.

April Rupert's first appearance in The *Sunday Express* - with the advent of the colour magazine.

October Publication of the first issue of the comic *Rupert Weekly,* edited by Leonard Matthews.

November Bestall Exhibition held at Fermoy Gallery, Kings Lynn.

9 December Terry Jones' documentary film 'The Rupert Bear Story : A tribute to Alfred Bestall" shown on Channel 4.

Rupert appears at Selfridges store, London in Father Christmas' grotto. It was very popular with queues lasting up to 2 hours.

1983

Followers of Rupert founded by Tony Shuker, who produced the first issue of *Nutwood - the Journal of The Followers of Rupert*.

Rupert's Fun and Puzzle Book published by Dean International for W.H.Smith.

Two Rupert Books in a box published by Octopus books for Marks and Spencer.

A re-recording of the Jackie Lee hit Rupert released by Rose Records. The song was sung by Tigerlily - alias 11 year old Tina Matania.

1984

Rupert is featured in literature provided for children by the British Diabetic Association.

Rupert Bear's Box (3 books) published by Methuen.

The Book of Rupert Favourites sold at British Home Stories featuring redrawn Mary Tourtel stories

The Rupert Treasury published by Purnell.

Some Adventures of Rupert published by Octopus Books.

September 15 First official gathering of the Rupert Followers, held at the Robin Hood Hotel, Newark-on-Trent. Alfred Bestall attended.

The same day *Rupert Weekly* ceases publication with issue number 100. It merges with *Story Land*, with Rupert still making an appearance.

December Paul McCartney's BAFTA award winning video Rupert and the Frog Song released. It quickly became the second most successful video ever, only being outsold by Michael Jackson. To accompany it the song 'We All Stand Together' (arranged by former Beatles A & R man, George Martin) is released and rises to number 3 in the British charts.

1985

A Bestall art exhibition held at the Barbican Centre, London.

Facsimile limited edition version of The New Adventures of Rupert 1936, published priced £4.95.

Paul McCartney's 'We All Stand Together' wins the Ivor Novello Award for the best film theme or song.

June Alfred Bestall awarded an MBE and receives congratulation from Prince Charles

Rupert carried piggy-back by a contestant in the London Marathon.

George Perry's *Rupert - A Bear's Life* published.

Visitor Information Centre, Canterbury 1990

1996

1989 Rupert Annual

1996 Rupert Annual

Flower Parade Spalding, Lincolnshire

1984

Rupert outside the Visitor Information Centre, Canterbury 1990. Unfortunately, he could not see very well and minutes later was taken to Canterbury Hospital after a van ran over his foot!

Ian Robinson and John Harrold with Paul and Neil Mattingly, 1990

Courtesy of David Rose

Watts with the Jazz Bassoon by Sarah Watts released on cassette and featuring six jazz pieces composed by Mike Hatchard entitled the Nutwood Suite. It was dedicated to Alfred Bestall.

Rupert Birthday Video published by Animated Expression with narration by Ray Brooks.

November Rupert Exhibition held at the Canterbury Centre, organised by Audrey Bateman.

December The mystery of Mr Bear's occupation dominated the letters page of the Guardian.

1986

15 January Alfred Bestall dies aged 93 at Wern Nursing Home.

Facsimile limited edition of More Adventures of Rupert 1937, published priced £5.75.

Ladybird books publish the *Frog Song* featuring colour illustrations from Paul McCartney's film and the words and music for the song 'We all stand together'. It is also published in audio cassette as a Tempo Talking Story.

Rupert's New Adventures published by Dragon Grafton.

1987

Sow N' Grow with Rupert published by Dragon Grafton. Each book contained a packet of seeds and growing instructions.

1988

Rupert Fun published by Express Books featuring games, stories and puzzles.

An attendance record-breaking exhibition on Rupert held at Canterbury Heritage Museum in Mary Tourtel's home town. The Kentish Gazette described the city as in a grip of Rupert mania. The Marlowe Restaurant sold a special red and yellow Rupert cake.

Canterbury shops devoted window

What makes Britain Great is our monarchy, democracy, roast beef and Rupert, but not necessarily in that order

John Beck

1991

Costumes for Rupert and the Green Dragon, designed by Susie Caulcutt, 1992

Rupert Air Balloon at Leeds Castle, Kent

Costumes for Rupert and the Green Dragon, designed by Susie Caulcutt, 1992

1993 Rupert Annual

London Marathon 1996

1991 Rupert Annual

City in grip of Rupert mania

RUPERT mania is gripping Canterbury as the city festival turns the spotlight on its famous furry son.

The spectacular Rupert Bear exhibition at the heritage timewalk museum in Stour Street has spaented its own mini-event.

One restaurant has come up with a Rupert Cake, while the tourist information centre has devoted its window to the cartoon character.

There is also a Rupert *[pictured here]*.

Rupert events take Canterbury by storm, 1988

All profits from sales of the limited edition card — available at the tourist information office in St Margaret's Street — will go to a special fund.

It seems likely that fund will be the start of a public appeal to get a more permanent reminder of Rupert in the city.

The timewalk museum's exhibition is undoubtedly the most comprehensive ever staged about the little character created by Canterbury artist Mary Tourtel.

The Daily Express has come up trumps by lending several original Rupert drawings from the pen of Mary's successor Alfred Bestall.

There are also rare editions of Rupert annuals and a mountain of memorabilia.

Items, like the

museum and will form the centre of its permanent Rupert collection.

Other items are on loan from Paul McCartney, the pop superstar who is arguably Rupert's best-known fan.

In addition to loaning original acetates from his Frog Song video, Paul has written the foreword to the exhibition's delightful colour programme.

"For the British, Rupert is an institution — like the Queen," writes Paul. "Britain just wouldn't be the same without him."

The exhibition, which is open daily including Sunday afternoons, has been sponsored by MIM Britannia, one of many companies which over the years have used the image of Rupert to sell their products.

The little chap has

A 1920 illustration of Rupert by Mary Tourtel when he looked more like a real bear.

notebooks to plates. But I doubt if there has been a stranger tribute than the gaudy cake at the Marlowes Restaurant in St Peter's Street.

The all-fruit concoction will

The first Rupert stamps published in Guernsey in 1993. Drawn by John Harrold

"I think I've got a lead on the Nutwood Beast"
Punch 1991

displays on the Rupert theme.

A runner dressed as Rupert runs the marathon raising money for muscular dystrophy.

1989 A facsimile limited edition version of The New Rupert Book 1938 published priced £6.75.

The BBC publish 4 books featuring adaptations of Bestall stories by Mike Trumble.

Rupert and Canterbury Group formed to produce commemorative plaques for buildings associated with Mary Tourtel. Three plaques, all featuring Rupert's image, were erected.

Ian Robinson joins the *Daily Express*.

October 18 Rupert - a comic is published by Celebrity Publications.

1990

Rupert writer James Henderson retires.

October Rupert comic ceases.

Ian Robinson and John Harrold visit Canterbury to sign Annuals.

1991

A new Rupert series shown on ITV.

1992

November 8 A Birthday lunch held by the Rupert and Canterbury Group.

Rupert used by Discover East Kent tourism project.

The Rupert Gallery opened at Canterbury Heritage Museum.

Rupert and the Green Dragon - a play for the stage produced by Layston Productions Ltd.

1993

Gina Hart first employed as a Rupert colourist. First Rupert stamps published in Guernsey, designed by John Harrold.

Courtesy of Julien Hooft Collection

Did you know there is a society dedicated to Rupert called **The Followers of Rupert**.

For membership details contact Shirley Reeves, 31 Whitely, Windsor SL4 5PJ

A statue in Rupert's honour would appeal to all generations and could become one of the most famous pieces of sculpture in the country. It would quickly challenge Sir George Frampton's famous bronze of Peter Pan in Hyde Park in popularity.

An ideal spot for him would be in the centre of a fountain, the water protecting him from mischief and attracting 'lucky coins' for charities. The site would probably need to be specially designed, perhaps in a new shopping complex, where Rupert could be protected by shopkeepers during the day, and locked at night, although preferably still seen. The outside of the fountain might contain high quality tiles with enamel images of most of the characters and the names of key illustrators and writers. John Harrold would be the ideal choice to design the statue and volunteered this quick sketch to help people visualize the scheme.

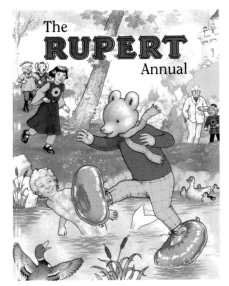

1997 Rupert Annual

It was Bestall who decided that Rupert's trousers should have exactly six stripes, so that there would be continuity when assistants were drawing other panels in a story

1995 Rupert Annual

Collector Peter Blackburn 1997

The Rupert Bear Collection of hand-numbered limited edition premier quality prints published by Hawk Books, 1997

1994
Bruintje Beer exhibition held at Teylers Museum, Haarlem.

1995
6 October Alex Cubie dies at Girvan.

Rupert's 75th birthday celebrations held at Canterbury.

Bethnall Green Museum of Childhood hold a 75th Anniversary Exhibition, which travels to other venues.

Rupert pasta, lemonade and party cakes unleashed on the world.

24 November The *Independent* prints an article by David J.Brazier arguing that Rupert once embodied Britain's moral spirit. Now the cartoon bear just reflects our loss of direction and has '*relinquished his grasp on the ethical nettle*'. A skilful reply in the bear's defence was swiftly published by Mr Victor Watson of Cambridge.

1996
9 March - 25 May Memorial exhibition of Alex Cubie's work held at the McKechnie Institute, Girvan.

Colourist Doris Campbell retires. Gina Hart takes over.

1997
A consortium of British animators, together with Gerry Anderson, the creator of the TV series Thunderbirds, apply for a £30 million lottery grant to make the first cinema feature on Rupert Bear. The application was not successful.

14 July Doris Campbell dies.

November The Rupert Bear Dossier published by Hawk Books.

Carole and Lawrence visiting Rupert at Canterbury Heritage Museum 1997

THE FUTURE..

95

Select Bibliography

R.Allen, *Voice of Britain: the Inside Story of the Daily Express*, 1983

Audrey Bateman, *The Caldwells of Canterbury: An Artistic Family*, Bygone Kent Vol 12 Number 4 pp 187-191

John Beck, *Mary Tourtel - Creator of Rupert Bear*, Book and Magazine Collector No.69, December 1989

John Beck, *Rupert Bear & Alfred Bestall*, Book and Magazine Collector No.94, January 1992

John Beck, *Rupert Books & Ephemera*, Book and Magazine Collector No.140, November 1995

Margaret Blount, *Animal Land,* 1974

Blue Peter Annual 1981 - The Bear Facts

Alan & Caroline Bott, *Alfred Edmeades Bestall, MBE 1892-1986 - An Exhibition of his paintings and drawings at Rake Court, Milford, Godalming, Surrey*, 1988

Caroline Bott, *Alfred Bestall*, The Antique Collector, April 1988 pp.80-85

Mary Cadogan, *Sixty Years in the Same Trousers,* Sunday Times 9 November 1980

Alan and Laurel Clark, *An interview with Alfred Bestall,* Golden Fun, Issue 12 1981.

Alan and Laurel Clark, *Mary Tourtel,* Golden Fun, Issue 15 1985.

Followers of Rupert, *Nutwood, Newsletter and Specials,* **from 1983 to present**

W.O.G.Lofts & D.J.Adley, *Collecting Rupert Bear*, Book and Magazine Collector No.5 July 1989

W.O.G.Lofts & D.J.Adley (revised and updated by John Beck), *The New Rupert Index*, 1991

Wilhelmina Ockenden, Obituary of Mary Tourtel, *Simon Langton Girls School Magazine*, July 1948

George Perry, *A Bear's Life - Rupert*, 1985

Brian Stewart & Audrey Bateman, Canterbury Heritage Museum exhibition catalogue, 1988

Teylers Magazijn No.43, Teylers Museum 1994

The Times 16 January 1986 - Alfred Bestall's obituary

Herbert Tourtel's Diary 1898-1900, Canterbury Museums collection.